NOT THAT I BRAG

BERYL KINGSTON

Not that I Brag. Paperback Version.
Copyright © Beryl Kingston 2022

All rights reserved.

No part of this book may be reprinted or reproduced or utilised in any form or by any electronic, mechanical, or other means, now known or hereafter invented, including photocopying and recording, or in any form of storage or retrieval system, without prior permission in writing from the publisher.

If you would like to share this book with another person, please purchase an additional copy for each recipient.

ISBN: 9798842548415

CHAPTER 1

They're sending me to a cattery! Me! The indignity of it! A cattery! If I hadn't heard it with my own sharp ears I'd never have believed it. I have the most acute hearing. Not that I brag. It's a fact of feline life, that's all. Or to be more accurate a fact of my particularly talented feline life. Acute hearing and a fine neat pair of ears. Jenny's always saying so. 'Haven't you got lovely ears darling,' she says. And then I narrow my eyes and smile at her to show her how sensible she's being, because for a human she's really not at all bad. If it had been left to her, there'd have been no consideration of a cattery.

It's all *his* fault. I realise that. She would never have done such a thing, if it hadn't been for him. She'd have taken me with her, the way she always does. We have an agreement about these things. That revolting cat-basket would be taken out of the loft and I would allow her to put me inside it. After a struggle of course. That's perfectly understood between us. No self-respecting cat ever obeys anyone straight away. It's not in our nature. A little preliminary spitting and snarling is expected of us. After all we're not dogs.

I knew we were in for trouble the minute she bought Him into the flat that night. *Not* a prepossessing creature. After years of living in my extremely handsome company I would have expected her to have better taste. But a gangly, uncoordinated animal like that! I could hardly believe my eyes. And I do have exceptionally good eyesight and the most beautiful yellow eyes. She's always saying so. 'Haven't you got beautiful yellow eyes my darling and all that lovely black fur,' she says, and I narrow my eyes and smile at her to show her how sensible she's being. His eyes are the most non-descript colour you could imagine. Not even blue. A sort of wishy washy grey which probably accounts for his excruciating eyesight. He can't see more than three inches in front of his nose, which incidentally is *not* a pretty sight either, long and bony and, as far as I can ascertain, totally devoid of any sense of smell. He had a dish of prawns right under his chin for nearly ten minutes on one occasion and didn't even twitch.

And now he has the effrontery to send *me* to a cattery. 'What are we doing with the mog?' he said. The mog!

I was lying among the cushions on her settee, which is the most comfortable place in the flat, so after I'd given him my most venomous hate-look with my eyes narrowed and my head absolutely still, I opened my eyes as wide as they would go and looked at her. I must say I expected her to be as upset as I was. But no, she put one of her paws on that horrible shaggy fur he has on his head and made her cooing noises, and didn't even look at me.

'I don't know darling,' she said. 'What do you think?'

'Send it to a cattery. I know a good one.'

It! I was so annoyed I had to leave the room.

And now that revolting basket is standing in the hall and one of those awful cars is standing in the road and they're both running from room to room, calling me. As if I'd answer, at a time like this! I've got myself a nice little hidey hole in the airing cupboard, right at the back behind the hot water tank. It's like a furnace in here, of course, but occasionally one simply has to suffer for one's rights. I'm certainly not going to a cattery without putting up a fight.

'Oh dear!' I can hear her saying. 'I can't find him. He couldn't have got out could he? Poor little thing!'

'Not past me!' he says. The arrogance of it! It makes my fur bristle. As if I couldn't outwit a creature like that!

'Perhaps we ought to cancel. Or go tomorrow. When he's got used to the idea. We can't just go off and leave him.' Now that's better. Now you're talking sense.

'The flight's booked. The hotel's paid for. We're not ruining our holiday for some cantankerous animal. He's in here somewhere. It's just a question of looking.' Cantankerous! I like that! He should talk, that way he runs about the place when he's in a bad mood.

'But what if we can't find him?'

'We'll find him, wretched thing. Think criminal!'

Oh that's nice! That's very nice! 'He's black, so where would a black cat hide? Somewhere pitch black, like a coal hole. Look under the beds.'

'I've looked.'

'Look again. Think. What's the darkest corner in the flat?'

I can hear her feet pattering towards the airing cupboard. Damn man! Why couldn't he have kept his mouth shut?

Well, I'm here, and it's every bit as bad as I expected. They put you in cages! Cages! I ask you! Rows and rows and rows of them, with an eighth-grade mouser in every single one. Not the right sort of place for an animal like me. I shall escape, of course, the very first chance I get. Oh, I'm glad I made them suffer on the journey. Jenny cried, tears in her eyes and sniffing and all that sort of stuff.

She was pretty near tears when she found me behind the hot water tank. 'Oh look,' she said, 'he's hiding away, poor thing. I'm sure he knows. Look at his poor little face.'

I gave her my pathetic look to encourage her and she picked me up and cuddled me under her chin, which was actually rather pleasant, because for a human being, she feels soft and smells quite nice. Not as nice as I do, of course, that goes without saying, but nice enough to make you want to purr. So I purred for a few minutes. She was pathetically grateful.

'It breaks my heart to send him away,' she said.

'Couldn't we take him with us?'

'No we could not.'

'He'd be ever so good.' I looked angelic and narrowed my eyes at her again. And then He actually had the effrontery to seize me by the scruff of the neck and hurl me into the basket, as if I were some sort of vegetable. I was so stunned, I didn't even have time to scratch him. He takes my breath away. Doesn't he know what sort of animal he's dealing with? Ignorant creature!

He didn't carry the basket any too gently either, even though she did try to warn him.

'Don't swing him darling. He hates being swung about. Oh look at his poor little face.'

'If you ask me, the sooner we get him to the cattery the better,' he said and he flung the basket into the back seat, so that I quite lost my balance. Only for an instant, of course, but it was very unpleasant. I need hardly tell you that no cat worth his salt would ever be seen losing his balance. It is quite the worst thing that could ever happen to a feline. We have absolutely perfect balance, when it isn't being interfered with.

Then the car began to roar and throw itself about the way it always does. That always makes me howl, even at the best of times, and this was quite definitely *not* the best of times, so I set up the most heart-rending caterwaul you have ever heard. She was so upset she cried all the way.

Not that it had any effect on *him*. 'It's only a cat

for God's sake,' he kept saying. 'Take no notice.'

It was a terrible journey. I made sure of that. She was still sniffing when the car stopped roaring and snarled to a halt.

'Let me take him in,' she begged.

He was foul to the last. 'No,' he said. 'I'll take him. You'll only get upset. He'll be all right.'

'Carry him gently then,' she said, giving me a watery smile. The treachery of it. You really would have thought she'd have put up more of a fight. What's the matter with her? I turned my back on the pair of them. There are times when the best thing is simply to show them how contemptible they are. If he was going to fling me about again, then I had no intention of letting him see my face. I shall escape from this place at the very first opportunity. They needn't think they can do this to me and get away with it.

Actually he didn't carry me far, which was just as well for he really is the clumsiest creature on two legs. I could hear bells ringing, at a distance, and then a gate creaking open and another man's voice speaking, but too softly for me to understand what he was saying. I'd have liked to look. But I have my pride.

Then the basket swung, once, and the gate creaked and I was being carried again. Only a great deal more gently. For a minute or two, I almost hoped Jenny'd got out of the car and taken over, but then I smelled a new human being, and I knew I must be inside the cattery and with someone else.

Now whatever I might think about catteries in general, I will say this for this cattery man, he smells extremely good, quite exciting in fact and certainly not human. Most humans only smell of soap and their awful sour sweat. *He* smells of that dreadful tobacco, the stuff he puts into a roll of paper and burns just inside his mouth, if you ever heard of anything so ridiculous. I can't smell tobacco on the cattery man at all, or soap, and only a trace of sweat which isn't unpleasant, but I can detect horses and donkeys, leather, compost, a whole variety of cats, of course, and cat's-meat and spearmint, and quite a lot of other things I haven't deciphered yet, so he's obviously a creature of taste.

And he carried the basket very smoothly. Better than Jenny does, to tell the truth. In fact for a human he would be really quite likeable if it wasn't for the fact that he lives in this awful place. He even held the basket steady while he unlocked the door to the second row of cages, which is rare in a human. When their forepaws are busy, they usually dump you down on the floor, right beside their clumsy feet. Which is *not* a pleasant place to be I do assure you.

'There you are,' he said, when he'd carried me inside. 'First rate accommodation for a first rate cat.' He set the basket down on a shelf, just about level with his jersey and bent down so that his face was quite close to mine and we could look at each other. But I notice he kept a respectful distance between us. And quite right too. 'Are you coming out to have a look round? Or do you want to stay in there for a little while?' A polite man, you notice. Knows how to talk to cats.

I decided to have a look round. So after a necessary pause, for no self-respecting cat ever rushes into anything, I stepped out of the basket, very gradually, of course, and delicately, so as to show him I wasn't approving of his cage, merely inspecting it. And I must say it really isn't at all bad. For a cage.

For a start it's on three levels. A tiled floor. Very clean. I like a clean floor. Then this shelf where he'd put that horrible cat-basket and then above that another shelf right underneath a window. I walked up the ramp to the top shelf to have a look out and I could tell at once that was where the donkeys were. I could smell them quite clearly, and dogs, and rabbits, and mice, and tall grass. A good place for hunting. It occurred to me that I might spend a little time hunting before I escaped. And then, good feline heavens, I noticed a mouse sitting right underneath my window, cleaning its whiskers. The effrontery! It made my fur bristle. That wouldn't have lasted a second I can tell you, if there hadn't been all that wire between us.

When I turned round to examine the rest of the cage, I had quite a surprise. The cat-basket was gone, good riddance to bad rubbish, and there were my own two bowls standing on the tiled floor, and my own bed tucked inside the house on the middle shelf. Well! How did he manage that? I was really quite impressed, especially as there was water in one bowl and some very strong smelling meat in the other, and quite palatable too. I tried it. After he'd shut the door and left me, of course, because it wouldn't have done to appear too keen.

I shall have a little rest, when I've cleaned my face and paws. Then I shall plan my escape.

Well I've been here several days now, and I must say it's not a bad place, taken all in all. The food is excellent, *and* served on time. No hanging about here. And the beds warm themselves up when it's cold, which is something any cat would appreciate, because we do like warmth.

It's been raining a lot. I've been up at the window watching it. So I've deferred my escape for the time being. Better to wait for an improvement in the weather. After all there's no rush. And when I break out, I'd like to do it in comfort and style. There's nothing stylish about wet fur. It looks revolting and feels worse. No, no I've plenty of time. I shall choose my moment. Meanwhile there's plenty of good food, and a comfortable bed to sleep in whenever I want to, and the howling, of course. I do enjoy the howling.

They're a very communicative lot in here. They howl and caterwaul at regular intervals all through the day, sending messages along the line and establishing rank order and that sort of thing. I have an exceptionally piercing howl, so it didn't take long to prove to them that I was the most important animal in our block. In fact I was leading the chorus on my very first day here. Which was only to be expected. The howl at daybreak is the best, I think. There is a tabby with three kittens in the end cage and she is a particularly sweet singer and very informative. Acts as look-out for the rest of us, and always gives me the most placating purr-talk. If it wasn't for the fact that I shall have to make a bid for my freedom sooner or later, I would actually rather like to see her.

The cattery-man has just come in. What's this he's putting in my bowl? It smells like rabbit.

It *is* rabbit. My whiskers, this is the life and no mistake.

The rain has stopped. It was rabbit again this morning, Delicious. I ate every last morsel. I shall plan my escape when I've had a little nap.

You'll never guess what's happened. They've come back. What do you think of that? On the very day I was going to break out too. Isn't that just typical? I had it all planned. The tabby at the end sang all clear, the sun looked as though it was set to shine for the rest of the day. It was the perfect opportunity. I was just washing my back, so as to be in perfect condition for the dash, when I heard a car approaching. Now I'd know the sound of His car anywhere, but really, if it hadn't been for the fact that I have perfect hearing, I'd have doubted the evidence of my own ears, sharp though they are. What on earth have they come back for so soon? Have they no sense of timing?

Of course it *was* them, and *He* was driving. I could tell that from the way the car scrunched to a halt and the way his feet came scrabbling out of it and the number of times he had to bang the door before he could get it to shut. He has no finesse, clumsy creature. I couldn't hear Jenny, which was rather a disappointment.

Then the outer door of my hut swung open and I could see that objectionable cat-basket swinging towards me and behind it the cattery-man treading softly and, behind the cattery-man, him, crashing about on those inelegant feet.

The cattery-man unlocked the door. 'I'll coax him, shall I?' he said. A sensible creature, the cattery-man.

'No,' he said. 'That's all right, thanks, I can manage him.' He grabbed me by the scruff of the neck and shoved me bodily underneath his arm, with one smelly hand clamped around my forepaws, which is not the most comfortable of positions, I can tell you, nor the most dignified.

I bore it until we were outside the hut and then I made a super-feline effort, tensing my back legs against his ribs, and sprang out of his grip into the air, giving his bare arm a nice long scratch as I went. I could hear him yelling behind me as I landed on the roof of the hut but there wasn't time to look back. The tree was immediately in front of me. With two graceful bounds I was across the roof and climbing the trunk. What a marvellous feeling! Bark under my claws and all the exciting scents of the open air in my nostrils and the thick cover of oak leaves rushing towards me as I climbed. That'll teach them to send *me* to a cattery!

Actually I went rather further up the tree than I'd intended, but it was a fine view and there was no way they could climb up after me and get me down. I sat in a fork and made myself comfortable and looked down to see what they were doing. He was examining his arm. What a wimp! And the cattery-man was looking rather worried. He was squinting up at me, and he'd taken off his cap to scratch his head. And there was Jenny, looking so upset, trying to see me through the mass of leaves. She's one of the nicer humans, but her sight isn't much good either.

'Oh, there he is!' she said. 'My poor boy. What did you do to frighten him so?'

'Do? I like that!' he said, rubbing his scratches. 'I didn't do anything, and he's scratched me half to death.' Good! I hope I have.

'We'll have to get him down,' she said, 'poor thing. Is he stuck do you think?' I blinked at her to comfort her, but I don't think she could see, because she looked more worried than ever. 'Come on, darling! Come down to mummy!' She's always saying silly things like that. It seems to please her and she means well. So I blinked at her again. But I didn't move, of course.

'Get a ladder!' He said to the cattery-man.

'No darling, not yet. Let me call him. I expect he's

frightened. You'll only make him worse with a ladder.'

'I'll make him worse with a half brick,' he said. You see the sort of man he is.

There was quite a long pause after that, and the cattery-man walked away behind the huts where I couldn't see him. I began to think it might be a good idea to descend. Not all the way to the ground of course. Not yet anyway. But down to a more reasonable height. There were two rooks circling the tree and they can be quite unpleasant if they've a mind to. Nasty beaks, rooks. I made a few tentative steps along the wider branch.

At that moment a breeze sprang up. Not a violent breeze, I'll agree, but enough to shake the bough I was crawling along. And the cattery-man returned with a ladder. Time to take action, I thought to myself, surveying the possibilities. I waited until the ladder was propped in position against the fork I'd just vacated, and then I set off.

Now, I don't know if you've ever noticed it, but climbing down is infinitely more difficult than climbing up. And of course this descent was made a great deal more difficult by the breeze I told you about and the fact that I really didn't know where they'd go moving that ladder next. I could hear it crashing through the foliage behind me. Very alarming, hearing a ladder crashing through the foliage just behind you. If they'd left me alone, and there hadn't been a breeze, I could have got down quite safely. It would have taken a little time, but I could have managed it, a cat with my sense of balance. But they would rush me. So it wasn't my fault that I lost my footing. I was feeling my way slowly when suddenly there was air under my feet instead of bark. I could feel myself falling and He was roaring and Jenny was screaming and a muddle of leaves and branches was flashing past my vision. Not a nice moment, I can tell you.

I managed to right myself in the air, the way we cats always do, and finished the fall feet downwards, ready to land. Which was some consolation. I made a good landing too, although I do say so myself, a soft landing, claws out, all four feet gripping. Excellent. The only trouble was I'd landed on one of the donkeys and the poor foolish creature was so frightened it kicked up its heels and set off round the field, braying and bucking for all it was worth. I only just had time to leap to the ground and make a bolt for it or I could have been caught a nasty blow from one of those hooves. Terrified donkeys have very little sense of direction. I ran like lightning and didn't stop until I was underneath the nearest cover, which turned out to be a car of some description. Very smelly and oily.

It took me quite a while to get my breath back and recover my equilibrium. I could see feet running about on the small pebbles in front of me and Jenny was scolding him, I was very glad to hear. 'Why couldn't you have left him alone? You know how sensitive he is. Poor little cat.' Presently I could see her feet walking towards the car and, after a pause, she knelt down in front of me and put her face right down almost onto the pebbles and looked under the car so that we could see one another.

'Come on,' she said, in her softest voice, holding out her fingers towards me under the car. 'I won't hurt you. Come on. Come on.' It was almost like a purr. I told you she was nice, didn't I.

Even so I took my time and inched out, very very slowly, because there was no knowing where those donkeys were or what He might do. Besides it's a matter of pride not to appear rushed or uncontrolled. She went on kneeling on the pebbles, making encouraging noises and holding out her hands. Even when I reached her and sniffed her finger tips just to make quite quite sure, she stayed still and didn't grab at me, so after a little while I crawled out into the sunshine and allowed her to pick me up. It was nice to be back with her again. I couldn't help purring. She stroked me all down my head and back and all round my ears, the way she does, and I nudged her chin and narrowed my eyes for her and purred louder than ever. Oh it *was* nice to see her.

She kept me on her lap all through the journey too, because she said I'd suffered enough. Which was true.

'Well don't blame me if it's sick,' He said. Stupid man. As if I'd be sick when she's stroking me. I don't think he's all there.

It was quite a pleasant journey, despite the roaring

and rattling about. But when we stopped we weren't at her flat. Now what?

We're in a strange house with its own front door and I think it belongs to him from the way he walks about in it, throwing his coat onto chairs and switching on noise machines and opening windows. He crashes everything he touches. Well I hope we aren't going to stay here long, that's all I can say.

And my food bowl's empty.

CHAPTER 2

This is a most peculiar house. I can't say I like it much and I don't think Jenny does either. She's been sighing rather a lot lately and that's a sure sign of discontentment in humans. He is being absolutely foul, swearing and shouting and banging things about all the time. It's *so* unnecessary. With any luck she'll get tired of him soon and then we can go back to the flat, which was a much better place. I can't think why we ever left it.

In the meantime I shall make the best of a bad job. We cats can be philosophical when it suits us. Although it won't suit me for very long because this isn't the sort of house anybody with any class or character would actually want to live in. And I do have a great deal of class and character. Not that I brag. A fact of feline life, that's all. She and I are streets above pokey little houses like this.

I've given it a thorough examination and it doesn't amount to *anything* I can tell you. At the top of the stairs it's very much like the flat. Only noisier. The number of noise machines that man possesses is quite ridiculous, besides being unnecessary. The first thing he does when he wakes up in the morning is to switch on at least three of them, a box that makes faces, a box that boils water and gives out a high pitched whistle, which is most unpleasant, and a box that buzzes. He's very fond of that one and spends a lot of time rubbing his face with it, which just goes to show how very unintelligent he is. No cat in his right mind would ever rub faces with a box, especially one that buzzes and doesn't smell of anything. Chair legs and banisters and empty shoes, yes, but buzzing boxes, very definitely no.

Still, there are one or two corners here that are not unpleasant, a patch of untroubled carpet between a window and a noise machine and a leather sofa I am not supposed to sit on, if you ever heard of anything so stupid, and a dresser that's quite comfortable and so smothered with clobber that no one can tell whether I'm sitting on it or not. The dresser drawers are pretty good snoozing places too, providing nobody goes shutting them, which I'm sorry to say, they often do. Humans are very thoughtless about drawers. It's a fact I've often noticed.

The best rooms are the two on the ground floor, where he says I'm not supposed to go, because that's where the food is. There's so much food in this house you wouldn't believe it, gallons and gallons of milk, butter in great slabs, jugs of cream, huge joints of meat, tubs full of fish, rows and rows of chickens all hanging up by their legs in a freezing cold room they always keep shut, which is rather unreasonable. I wouldn't take much and they've got plenty.

The other room downstairs is full of tables piled

with food and chairs squashed under humans eating it, and a pretty horrible sight that is. So unnatural. Quite the most ridiculous method of transferring food from plate to palate that anyone ever devised, poking it into your face on the end of a metal stick. One or two of them manage it quite delicately. Jenny does for example. She's quite neat about it really. But most of them are coarse and clumsy. And the front room humans are the worst I've ever seen.

They make the most appalling noise too, a sort of nasal baying, 'H'yaw h'yaw h'yaw!' like donkeys. Most unattractive. And they all look alike, which is only to be expected I suppose since they all belong to the same family. I know that because when any of them arrived he always says, 'Here come the Yuppies, heaven help us!'

And Jenny says, 'At least they pay.'

Then He snorts down that long nose of his and says, 'Sting 'em eh?' Although he never does. I've watched him very closely and I've never seen him sting anybody. In fact I don't think humans possess stings. It would be altogether too civilised for them, great crude clumsy things that they are. He just fancies himself, that's all it is. Bragging. He will keep saying he's watching me 'like a hawk'. A hawk! I ask you! Have you ever *seen* a short-sighted hawk? Although I must admit He *does* watch me. It's 'Where's that damn cat?' every other minute of the day, and 'You haven't let the cat in have you?' and 'I will *not* have animals in my kitchen'. Which is pretty rich when you consider that his kitchen is absolutely swarming with animals, morning, noon and night. Most of them distinctly unappetising specimens like humans and mice and cockroaches. He's so ridiculous I sometimes wonder if He knows how stupid he is. Ah well! It's not every animal lucky enough to be as intelligent and as beautiful as we are.

And He needn't think He can keep me out of anywhere.

Well I got in. I like a challenge. It's quite a good place. I suppose that's why He wanted to keep me out of it. Perverse you see. But *not* intelligent. He was actually banging out of the door when I slipped in. They'd left one of the windows open. Just a crack but it was enough. I'm very agile. Like greased lightning, Jenny always says. Anyway I was through that gap in less time than it takes to blink and slithering down the glass towards a work-top covered in fish. Imagine it! Lying there in lovely slimy heaps with their eyes glazed and their barbels sticking up like whiskers. Trouble was they were all too big and I didn't have time to sniff around for pieces. The place was full of humans you see and you can never be absolutely sure what any human being is capable of doing. Not on first acquaintance anyway. So I hid.

There was a convenient space in a cupboard underneath the work-top. Not particularly comfortable because there were rather a lot of saucepans in there and saucepans are always so knobbly, but dark, and the door was off its hinges, which was another advantage. Humans are a bit too prone to go shutting cupboards when you're still inside them. But I told you that before didn't I.

Luckily these humans were much too busy to shut anything. And so noisy. Banging frying pans and saucepans, clunking dishes, roaring ovens, slapping those fish about, and shouting and whistling all the time. Made me wince. But I stayed where I was and endured it because I knew it was only a matter of time before they started to drop things.

I was right, of course. I always am. Not that I brag. The first thing that fell was a sliver of that very tasty pink fish they call salmon. It landed in front of my cupboard. All I had to do was stretch out a paw and sneak it in. It was delicious. After that it snowed good things. Shreds of plaice, two more slices of salmon and a fine chunk of cod, enough to chew on for several minutes.

But then I heard one of them say something that made me put my ears right back.

'That cat's in here, Leroy. Eatin' the bits.'

I sat quite still and waited to see what would happen next, thinking that I might have to make a dash for it.

Another voice spoke. Quite a good voice, I thought, warm and drawly, a purring sort of voice.

'What you want, man? He no trobble. Let he alone.'

And a hand reached down into my hidey-hole and

tickled me under the chin. An excellent hand. The best I've ever smelt and I've smelt some pretty ripe ones. There were traces of roast meat on it, three different kinds of fish, cream, butter and a lot of other things I'd have recognised given just a little more time. I could have breathed in that combination for as long as he liked. But that wasn't all. Besides being a treat to the nostrils, that hand was a really good colour. Not ebony like me, of course. I wouldn't expect that. In fact I doubt whether any human being could equal my superlative colour. But close. A rich dark brown with a good sheen to it.

Now I don't know if you've noticed but most humans are an awful colour. A sort of wishy-washy pink like pork. And some of them don't have any colour at all, just a nasty grey. So you can imagine how pleased I was to see that hand. It made me wonder what the rest of him was like. So I stretched out my neck and leant out of the cupboard to see.

He was the most feline person I'd ever seen in my life. A long lean man, with an easy spine and a way of walking that was a joy to watch, rolling on the balls of his feet, instead of slap-slap flat like most of them do. And what a catty face! Broad forehead, long wide nose, sharp little teeth, round glass in front of both his eyes and a mane of hair, bushing out all around his face, thick and bristling and absolutely black. I liked him at once.

'Hello dere, cat,' he said. And he picked up a shred of chicken and dangled it right into my mouth.

I had a very good morning. I ate so much my belly was as tight as a drum, which is a marvellous feeling I can tell you. And when I simply couldn't eat any more, not even salmon, my friend Leroy held the door open so that I could stroll upstairs and sleep it off.

And the beauty of it is, *He* didn't know anything about it.

This place improves. He doesn't get any better, of course. You can't expect miracles. But there are plenty of other people here and some of them aren't bad. Take Leamington Spa, for instance.

She's little and quiet and old and she comes in twice a week and eats the roast-of-the-day. I know that because He always says, 'Here comes Leamington Spa,' in his sneering voice. 'Roast-of-the-day, what d'you bet?'

And Leamington Spa squeezes herself into the chair in the corner and puts her napkin across her knees and waits. The first time I saw her I knew she was intelligent and kind and likely to give me tit-bits if I asked her prettily enough. So I sat under the table and waited till his big feet had trodden out of the room and then I jumped up onto the chair beside hers and gave her my most loving look.

'You're a nice little cat, aren't you,' she said. So I was right about her intelligence.

Then she stroked me very gently across the head and neck, so I was right about her being kind.

But it took quite a long time to purr the food off

her plate. She eats very slowly, chewing a great deal, with her jaws rocking from side to side and a far-away expression in her eyes. But I reckoned she'd be worth waiting for, and so she was. It was cold, of course, and rather congealed and I had to take it under the table to eat it because He'd just come back into the room. But I had established a precedent.

The next time she came in I went straight to her table and sat in the chair opposite hers so that she could see at once that we would be having dinner together.

She was pleased to see me. I could tell that from the tone of her voice. 'Well hello, little cat. You're getting to be quite a friend of mine,' she said. 'What have they got to offer us today?' Us, you notice. Not me. I told you she was kind.

It was roast beef and rather stringy which was a bit of luck because she couldn't chew it very well so quite a lot of it got passed down to me. I would have had it all if it hadn't been for him, oozing across the middle of our excellent arrangement with a cloth over one arm and that silly false smile on his face.

'Is that cat annoying you, madam,' He said. Oh he's got no class at all. As if I'd annoy anybody. As if I could.

Leamington Spa was a match for him. 'Oh no,' she said, looking up at him mildly. She has a soft face despite her whiskers, which are haphazard but quite bristly. 'Oh no. He's no trouble. I like the company.'

'If he's a nuisance, you've only got to say and I'll

have him kicked out.' You see the sort of man he is. He can't even understand a little old lady. Kicked out indeed!

Didn't get him anywhere though because the minute his back was turned she dropped me a huge piece of meat, dripping gravy.

It's been very hot for the last few days. I don't mind the heat, of course. We cats are able to cope with most things. Unlike humans who complain at the least change. They've had all the kitchen windows wide open. Not that I worry about windows now either. Leroy always lets me in through the door.

The eating room has been more like an oven than the oven. And crowded with people. That Yuppie family is enormous. And their loud talk is worse in the heat.

'I *couldn't* take a holiday *now*, darling. With all the oiks on holiday! You must be joking.'

'Actually my cousin is lending me his yacht.'

'My mater's in Antibes.'

'God, this heat is *killing*!'

Jenny's been carrying food in and out from the kitchen to the eating room. It's the first time she's done it since we arrived and it's making her look very hot and harassed. She doesn't like doing it, although I notice that she tells him she does, 'No, no, darling. It's quite all right. I don't mind helping out.'

I know better, of course. I can always tell when she's lying. She puts on a look. Deliberately. I could tell you the actual moment when she starts to arrange it on her face. When she's really happy she never smiles like that.

He knows she's lying too. He says things in his false voice, like, 'I must make a special fuss of you.' Oh yes? I could tell him what he ought to do. Let her sit down for five minutes and have a rest. Or, 'What would I do without you?' I know what he'd have to do without her. He'd have to do all the work himself, lazy slob.

She goes on running about for him with her hair standing on end with grease and nasty little cuts on her fingers and her clothes all stained with sweat. I don't know when he imagines we're supposed to have any time together. I haven't sat on her lap for weeks! It's just as well I've got Leroy and Leamington Spa.

Well you'll never guess what's happened now. He's seen one of the mice. Oh he *is* quick! Like lightning! They've been here for months. I wonder he couldn't smell them. No sense of smell, that's his trouble. I told you that, didn't I.

Anyway, he's been running around all day squawking like a chicken, 'We've got mice! Mice! We shall be ruined! What if the inspector comes? Oh God, mice in *my* kitchen!'

I sat in the window seat and watched him for as long as I could bear it which wasn't very long I can tell you. Human hysteria gets very wearing very quickly. But when I got up and stretched myself ready to stroll away from it all, He suddenly went quite berserk, grabbed hold of me by the scruff of the neck as if I were a kitten or paralysed or something, and lifted me up in the air, shouting 'This is it! This is it!' I was *not* pleased. I put my ears right back and narrowed my eyes till I could barely see anything at all and swore at him in my most menacing way, deep down in my throat and baring my teeth. He didn't even seem to notice. There are times when I really wonder whether he can see anything at all. And I'm sure he's deaf.

'This is it!' He roared. 'We'll lock this damned cat in. Let him sort it out. You're always telling me what a marvellous mouser he is. Now we shall see.'

I couldn't believe my ears. He's spent all this time kicking me out of the place and roaring and carrying on about not having animals in his kitchen and now He wants me to stay there all night and catch mice for him. In this heat too! The effrontery of it! No mention of reward you notice. No 'Could you fancy a nice little bit of plaice?' or 'Would you like some cream you marvellous cat?' Oh no! Just, 'Let him sort it out.'

Well I won't do it. A cat has his pride.

I've been in this kitchen for hours and hours, and it's *not* a good place to be in the middle of the night, I can tell you. For a start there's nowhere to sleep. All the cupboards are full of saucepans and all the drawers are full of knives and the worktops smell of some sort of vile disinfectant. It's absolutely stifling in here. I wonder the mice don't die of asphyxiation. I've made myself a nest of sorts in a box half-full of paper towels, but it isn't the sort of place a cat of my calibre should ever have to endure. Well I ask you! Paper towels! Common paper towels! I shan't be able to sleep, of course, but at least it's away from the stink of that disinfectant.

I've just been woken up by the sound of scrabbling and scampering. The place is full of mice. Climbing up the legs of the tables and running in and out of the cupboards and squeezing themselves through the smallest cracks, which is quite amazing because they're very fat. They've obviously been living really well in this kitchen and for a jolly long time, if I'm any judge. Which, I hardly need tell you, I am. They're pretty dumb though, One of them's been sitting right alongside this box for ages. I could catch him in a snatch, if I wanted to.

I've just killed that mouse. Well the stupid thing was asking for it, sitting there preening its stupid whiskers right under my nose. I had it so quickly it didn't know what had hooked it. One flick of the paw, jugular bitten, finished. The beauty of it is, the rest of them didn't notice. They're still scrabbling about, twitching and darting in and out of cupboards as if this was just any other night, moronic creatures. I could catch the lot of them, if I wanted to.

I've had a magnificent night. There are corpses all

over the kitchen. Now I'm having a bit of a breather. Just for a moment, you understand, while I consider which of them I shall eat. I'm not exhausted or anything like that. Oh no, no, no. It was splendid sport. Most exhilarating. I'm a magnificent hunter. Not that I brag. A fact of feline life that's all. All cats hunt well but I hunt superlatively. It's all a question of timing you see and my timing is faultless.

I sat on a shelf as still as a stone until there were about a dozen grey backs bundling about right below me and then I dropped down on them so quickly I'd caught four of them before they could run. What a panic there was! Mice in every direction, running up chairs and over tables and into each other. Not that it made any difference. I picked them off wherever they went. One stupid thing tried to crawl up a tap. As if that would do it any good! I had it out by its tail, at once. And the two climbing up the window frame. Oh what slashing and scratching! What nipping and biting! Glorious! I haven't had such a triumph in months.

I shall clean my paws in case there are any of them left and they dare to come back. Cleanliness must be absolute if you mean to hunt with any sort of precision. Then I shall have a short nap which I richly deserve. Then I shall lay out the bodies.

He says he's 'Over the moon!' whatever that might mean. 'Over the moon! Fan-dabby-dozey! What a mouser!' On and on and on, over and over again, running round the kitchen picking up dead mice by their tails, and incidentally making a fine mess of my well-ordered lines, but I suppose that's only to be expected. 'What a mouser!'

He actually managed to get up early this morning. For once. He was in the kitchen before Leroy, and that takes some doing. I think he'd come down to catch me asleep and with no mice caught because He was *so* surprised when He saw the corpses his jaw dropped several inches, and a hideous sight that was, I can tell you. But then he got ridiculous of course and started running around screeching and laughing and throwing mice about and it wasn't long before people came jostling in to see what the row was about.

So now I'm the hero of the hour, she's cuddling me like baby and says I'm to have cream for my breakfast. And so I should think.

Now perhaps we shan't have quite so much nonsense about keeping me out of the kitchen. Or anywhere else for that matter.

CHAPTER 3

I have decided that the time has come to take Him in hand. He can't go on in that maladroit way forever, and as it looks as though we're going to stay here, more's the pity, something will have to be done. I shall begin by showing him the correct way to wash. His ablutionary style is crude in the extreme, no grace or style about it whatsoever. He just fills a bowl full of steaming water and throws it at his face. I ask you!

Well, that was a waste of time. And after I'd given him such a splendid demonstration too. I came up into their bedroom as soon as their bell machine started to rattle and sat in the middle of the carpet so that he couldn't help noticing. Then I went through the whole routine, slowly and really quite beautifully, washing my face with a curved paw, cleaning between my toes, biting out my fleas, very neatly and delicately of course, showing him the leg of mutton stance, even demonstrating the full sweep from the nape of my neck to the base of my tail. The works. They both watched me. I will say that for them.

'I think it's so clever,' Jenny said, 'the way they wash themselves.'

He just grunted. He's so uncouth.

'He's making his fur gleam,' she said. 'All down his back. Look at that.'

'It's a wonder he doesn't dislocate his neck,' He said, squinting at me.

'But don't you think it's clever?'

'Um.' He swung those bony legs out of the bed and yawned and scratched his head until his fur stood on end. Then he stumbled off to switch on all his other noise machines.

I was jolly tired by then, I don't mind telling you. Thorough ablutions are really quite exhausting. But I followed him into the washing room to see what he'd do. And you'll never believe it! After all that effort, he hadn't learnt a thing. He just filled the bowl and flung the water about exactly the same as ever. In fact, if anything, worse.

I was so cross with him I went straight downstairs with my tail in the air. I never met a creature so idiotic. And she likes him! There's no sense in the world.

So I didn't see Jenny get up. I wish I had because I'd have known at once that this was a different sort of day and I could have made a fuss of her, a bit of head-butting and purring or something like that, just to show her what an affectionate animal I am and stop her from looking so harassed.

As it was, she was down in the kitchen and fully dressed in her sensible clothes before I knew anything about it, pouring boiling water into a pot and burning bits of bread. They always *burn* their food. It's another one of their peculiarities. Anyway the sensible clothes alerted me at once. Something was up.

They spent most of the meal shouting at one another and dropped two pieces of burnt bread on the floor and turned on another noise machine that played his awful banging music so loudly it made my ears ache. Then she gave a shriek and grabbed a bag full of books from the sideboard and rushed out of the room, yelling, 'Oh God! I shall be late. See you tonight.' Humans really are the most agitating creatures. Never still for one minute. I think I shall find a nice sunny spot by the window and have a short snooze.

It's been a really boring day and they've all forgotten to feed me. She didn't come back and Leroy didn't come in so there was no fish at lunchtime. And there were only a couple of dark suited men in the dining room and a fat lot of good they were. Left half the food on their plates and then ruined it by smoking their horrible fire-sticks all over it. No self-respecting cat could have touched such an obnoxious mixture, I can tell you.

So I was pretty hungry by mid-afternoon - and bored, because He's no company for a cat at all. He's either rushing about roaring or lying flat on his back on the sofa fast asleep with his mouth open. Uncouth creature.

So I decided I might as well stroll out into the yard and see if there was anything interesting out there. But there wasn't. Not even the odd bone or a fish-head or two, and the dustbin lids are clamped down so tightly I doubt if even Leroy himself could have opened them. Nothing in the next two yards along either. I was getting hungrier and hungrier by the minute.

There's never any point trying the fourth yard along because there's a dog in there, a mean unpredictable thing, hates cats. So I took a turn up the alley, which is not a particularly nice place either, being dark and damp and full of broken glass and filthy paper and decaying cardboard. But preferable to bad-tempered dogs. At the far end of the alley there's a low wall which is quite a good spot for sunning yourself. If you can't eat, you might as well sit in the sun.

There are always lots of humans out there, charging up and down on the pavement or climbing in and out of their cars. And if you want to see something really grotesque, try watching that for a minute or two. The way they twist their bodies and grab the doors and wave their great feet in the air. Totally lacking in grace or control. They've got no idea how to fold their legs, for a start, and none of them know how to fall on their feet. I can't watch them. It upsets my sense of decorum. I curl up on the wall and close my eyes and let the sun polish my fur and try to pretend they're not there. Much the best way, I can tell you.

So you can imagine how surprised I was when

somebody came right up beside me and started to stroke my head. I knew who it was, of course, even with my eyes shut, because I could smell eau-de-cologne and moth-balls. It was dear old Leamington Spa.

'Hello Cat,' she said, when I opened my eyes. 'Come to tea have you?'

That was much more promising. I uncurled at once and stretched my spine ready to jump down. She opened a little creaking gate in the wall and went hobbling up the garden path towards the house. Not a very beautiful house. The paint on the windows is so old it's falling off in great grey-white flakes, and there are positive pits in the stucco. Still food is food, wherever it comes from. So I followed her.

She took an age to open the door, fiddling with the key and muttering to herself. In the end I had to call to her to remind her what she was doing or we would have been there all day. 'Yes, yes,' she said. 'Soon be there cat.'

There turned out to be one room at the end of a corridor. Not a bad place, taken all in all. No carpet on the floor, only some ancient lino which is very cold underfoot, but an excellent bed in one corner, all dips and hollows and heaped with pillows, and an old fashioned kitchen table full of plates and saucepans, all clean, which was rather a disappointment, and a huge armchair full of cushions and newspapers, pulled up right in front of one of those heat machines in the wall. She lit it with a match the minute we got into the room, even before she'd taken off her hat and coat. A creature of sense old Leamington Spa.

Tea turned out to be a tablespoon of milk in a saucer set down beside her chair while she drank that dark brown boiling water from a cup. I could really have done with a plate of boiled fish or the off-cuts from a joint or something sustaining like that, but anything is better than nothing.

It took her such a long time to get it ready that was the only trouble. I sat on her rug before the heat machine and waited as patiently as I could. But when she poured milk into a little green jug, my hunger pangs were so excruciating I had to cry a little.

'Oh you poor old Cat,' she said. 'Are you starving to death? I know how it feels.' She poured some of the milk into a saucer. I could hear it falling, blob, blob, and presently the gold-edged rim descended into my line of vision and I was able to break my long fast at last. It was blissful. I licked up every last drop and polished the saucer and gave my whiskers a most satisfactory wash. Oh a very pleasant creature, old Leamington Spa. Knows how to treat you.

By the time I was quite comfortable she'd finished her boiling water and was sitting quietly in her armchair in a cushiony sort of way with a good expanse of lap ready for me. So I jumped up, and after turning once or twice to shape a nest, I found a comfortable position and the two of us settled down for a little nap. Not a bad way to spend an afternoon.

*

By the time I got back to the restaurant, they'd started serving dinner and Jenny was home again, sitting at the table in their living room with the picture machine playing in the corner, soundlessly for once, and a red pen in her hand.

She was quite pleased to see me, which was gratifying. 'Where've you been?' she said, picking me up and cuddling me under her chin. 'I thought we'd lost you.'

I purred to show her she hadn't and she kissed the top of my head and put me down on the table beside a great pile of flat books. So then I knew where she'd been. It's a place called 'school'. She goes there quite a lot, and comes home smelling of dust and old rubber shoes and saying she's worn out. I think it's a place where they make those flat books, because she's always got piles and piles of them in her bag and she has to look at them and write on them in the evening, which is a good idea because it means she's sitting more or less still and I can settle down on her lap.

He doesn't like it, of course. But when did He ever like anything sensible? He's been perfectly revolting this evening, running up and down the stairs every five minutes, bellowing, 'Are you going to come and help me?' and 'How do you imagine I'm going to manage if you sit up here all the time?'

'It's your restaurant,' she said, the fifth time He appeared. She was looking at the books and stroking me round the ears. 'I've got my own job to do now. I don't mind helping out in the holidays. You know that. But term time's different.'

'Oh that's lovely!' he shouted. 'I thought we were building up this business together. Wasn't that what you said? Building up the business together. For our future.'

What a foul bully He is. Go on, I urged her, giving her my most loving look, fight back. Tell him you won't move.

But she gave in to him. 'Oh all right,' she said, and she sounded so weary. 'I'll just finish this lot and then I'll be down.'

He changed his tone a bit then. Went all oily. 'You know how it is, don't you darling. I don't mean to nag,' Oh no! Not much! 'Only this is so important.' So is cuddling me, you oaf!

But she put me down and followed him out of the room. Oh what a fool she's being. Can't she see He's the sort of creature you mustn't ever obey? They get worse if you give them their own way all the time. And just as she was beginning to act sensibly too.

Still at least there'd be food in the kitchen. So I took myself off there and dined quite well even though Leroy still wasn't back.

I don't think much of this school place. For a start it makes far too many books. She's always looking at them, when she isn't running in and out of the eating room waiting on the Yuppies. She laughs at them sometimes and reads bits out of them and laughs again, but when she's finished writing in them and they're all back in a neat pile on the table, instead of getting up and feeding me, she curls up on the sofa and goes to sleep. It is *not* good.

Leroy's back, but he's always busy too. It's just as well I've got old Leamington Spa to give me tea now and then, or malnutrition would be setting in. I shall probably stroll up and see her later this afternoon. It's a chilly sort of day and her room is usually warm

It started to drizzle the minute I'd settled down on the wall to wait for old Leamington Spa. I told you it was a foul sort of day didn't I. I had to get down pretty quickly and find somewhere dry or my fur would have been ruined. Not that you get a lot of choice in that little garden. It's either a rather dead-looking magnolia or a very dusty privet hedge. I chose the hedge because it does give better cover when it's wet, even though it's horribly dirty, and besides it's closer to the road, so I can keep a sharp look-out for the old lady, and be on that doorstep before her, ready and waiting to be let in. She likes me to welcome her.

She took an age to arrive this afternoon. I'd been sitting under the hedge for hours and hours before I heard her limping up the road towards me, muttering to herself, the way she always does. I darted across to the door and sat up and looked pretty, ready to greet her. And we ran into the house together to get out of the rain.

By that time the damp was really getting to me. I'd had to bristle my fur right up to keep warm. So I went and sat by the heat machine and looked hopeful.

'Throwing out hints eh?' she said, feeling along the mantelpiece for her box of fire-sticks and the matches. She lit one as she was struggling out of her wet coat and then held it in the corner of her mouth, trailing blue smoke, while she filled the kettle and made the heat machine go bang. It always goes bang before the flames rise inside their little white columns. Rather alarming the first time, I must admit. Now of course, I don't take any notice of it. I just sit tight on the rug and wait for the warmth to begin and the milk to be poured. What with the long wait and the drizzle I was good and ready for my milk this afternoon.

After she'd drunk her tea, she lit another fire-stick and we settled down for our afternoon nap, all warm and cosy. The same as usual.

I don't know how long I slept. The room was certainly appreciably darker when I woke, but that wasn't what woke me. It was the smell of burning, that hot prickling smell, very alarming. I sat up at once, instantly alert and ready to jump out of harm's way, which was just as well because the fire was just underneath my back paws. I saw it at once, a brown singed bit on Leamington Spa's skirt, very smelly and growing by the minute. I was off her lap and heading for the door in less than a split second I can tell you.

But the door was shut tight. I tried digging at it with all four paws, but I couldn't even dislodge the lino, and black smoke was billowing up from the rug all the time and making me sneeze. I tried lifting it, but I couldn't get my paw underneath. I tried kicking it, but that wasn't any good at all. And finally, when there were flames licking up the walls in the most alarming way, I put my head down as close to the crack in the wainscot as I could get it and howled and howled.

To my great relief, that did the trick. I could hear people crashing about outside the door and shouting, so I howled again to make them hurry up. It was getting uncomfortably hot in that room, I can tell you, and the fire was only inches away from my tail. But at last they got themselves organised. I could hear them hacking at the door with an axe, so I moved out of the way, just a little, in case they hacked me.

The door fell in all of a sudden and the fire made a noise like some great wild beast roaring and then rushed towards me, hissing sparks. I was off out of that room quick as a lick, dodging between their ungainly legs and pelting down the corridor and out into the cool air. What a relief! I'm not a coward. Cats are always incredibly brave. That's how we are. But that fire really was a bit much and humans are so slow when you want them to do something useful.

I sat under the privet hedge in the dark for a little while, cleaning my fur and getting my breath back but close enough to the road to run if I needed to, so I had a good view of everything that was going on. Now I was out of it, I must say it was really quite entertaining. There were people rushing in and out of the house carrying axes and blankets and boxes and babies, and an absolutely goggle-eyed crowd standing around on the pavement saying 'Oooh' and 'Aaah' and 'Who'd have thought it?' and herds of cars cruising by very slowly so as to get a good view.

Presently there was a terrible clanging of bells and I could hear tyres squealing and a huge red car drove right up on the pavement, scattering the crowd to right and left, and half a dozen huge men jumped out and began to play some sort of game with a hose, unwinding it and running up the street with it calling to one another as they went. Human beings are very peculiar sometimes. Very big men, they were, and all wearing yellow hats and baggy yellow trousers. So perhaps it was some sort of carnival. By now I was enjoying myself, so I sat tight and watched to see what would happen next.

And all sorts of things happened. All at once. It was rather confusing. First of all Jenny came pushing through the crowd, right to the front, and obviously looking for me. But just as I was inching my way out of the privet to talk to her, another large car arrived on the pavement. This was white with a blue light flashing on its roof and everybody stood aside for it, so I lost sight of her. Two men in green suits got out and took a bed made of metal sticks out of the back of the car and pushed it into the house. Now that I was out of the hedge I could see that there was a lot of dirty water slopping out of the front door and trickling down the path towards the crowd, so there must have been a flood in there as well as a fire. What a good job I managed to get out.

Then I heard Jenny's voice saying. 'There's our cat! Look!' and He appeared out of the crowd and picked me up by the scruff of the neck and swung me in the air. It was extremely undignified, but before I had a chance to scratch him, Jenny's hands had reached up caught me and she was cuddling me under her chin and telling me I was her beauty.

While I was enjoying a little well-earned admiration a man's face suddenly mooned in on me, grinning.

'That cat's a hero,' he said. And the faces all round us turned and stared at me. 'A hero!'

Well of course.

'D'you mean the mice?' He said, putting on his proud look. Annoying creature! You'd think he'd caught them.

'Mice?' the man said. 'What mice? No, no. I mean the fire. Saved an old lady from burning, that cat of yours. Ought to have a medal.'

'I knew it,' Jenny said, holding me so tightly it was really quite uncomfortable. 'I knew he'd done something marvellous. I could tell it. Didn't I say so the minute I saw him? What did he do?'

'Raised the alarm,' the man said, tickling me under the chin. 'Not a minute too soon either. Old lady was asleep you see. If it hadn't been for your cat missus, the whole darn place would've gone up in smoke. That animal's a giddy marvel. That's what he is. A giddy marvel.'

Well of course I've always known that. But it's nice to hear it said now and then. I preened a little and looked pretty because I could see that all those faces were admiring me and you have to play to your audience.

Then another man pushed forward out of the crowd with an odd-looking black box hanging round his neck, which he pointed at me, I can't think why. All it did was to flash once all of a sudden like an eye and I really couldn't see the point of that. But it pleased Jenny and He was full of himself, grinning and laughing his silly laugh as if he was the hero and not me. Aggravating creature.

Then the two men came walking out of the house towards us, pushing that metal bed between them. And Leamington Spa was lying on the bed all wrapped up in a blanket with her eyes shut. They put her in the white car while all the people in the crowd pushed forward to get a good look at her and Jenny said, 'Poor old thing. I do hope she'll be all right.' And He said, 'They're as tough as nails these old things. You don't want to worry about her.'

Then the white car drove away with its blue light going round and round and flashing all the time and when it had gone the whole place was suddenly much darker and the excitement was over.

'Let's go home,' Jenny said. 'We can't do anything more here.' And she carried me back to the restaurant. About time too.

They gave me salmon for dinner. So I must be a hero. But I noticed He wouldn't let me sleep on their bed. Can't have everything I suppose and I'm so tired after all my exertions, I could sleep anywhere. I wonder where they've put old Leamington Spa.

CHAPTER 4

He's gone mad. Stark, staring, raving, totally, absolutely bonkers. Just when I'd got the kitchen situation all sorted out to my satisfaction, he's stopped cooking and thrown away all the food. I went down this morning, in the usual way, to see what Leroy had for my breakfast, and the place was bare. No Leroy, no fish, no dish of cream, nothing. To a cat of my intelligence it really is incredible that any creature could be so foolish. What does he think he's playing at?

I hung around for quite a long time, just in case it was all a mistake, but nothing happened. No sign of anyone. Not even him. It's jolly cold in an empty kitchen I can tell you. In the end I gave up and went back upstairs.

Jenny'd gone rushing off to that school place, hugging that great heavy bag of hers, with her scarf trailing behind her and her beret over one eye, so the flat was nicely empty and still warm. She'd left a heap of that awful tinned cat-food in the corner, so I ate some of it, just to show willing because she means well. Besides, there wasn't anything else. Then I walked through into their living room and jumped up on the windowsill where there's a nice patch of sun.

And would you believe it? He'd moved that too. There wasn't a hint of any sunshine anywhere in the room. I know because I looked. It just shows how malevolent He is.

In the end I gave up the search and came back to the windowsill. There's a good view of the street from up here, if nothing else, and we cats like to watch the world go by. Keeping an eye on things is one of the activities we're particularly good at. It's because we've got such splendid eyesight I daresay, and the capacity to sit absolutely still for hours and hours. Which is more than can be said for most human beings.

Actually I didn't have to sit still for more than a minute or two before a white van drew up beside the front door immediately below me and two men in boiler suits got out. He must have been watching for them because he was out on the pavement and talking to the first one before the second had walked round the van. Very animated conversation, too, lots of head nodding and hand shaking. Then they all came tramping into the house. I could hear their feet from where I sat. Most intriguing.

Now what? I thought. So I went downstairs to find out.

The ground floor was full of machines all wobbling about in the most ridiculous way and making a great deal of unnecessary noise. I can't stand machines. They're even worse than humans, and that's saying something. There were two of them in the eating room, bouncing about over the carpet spitting out dust. Machines, I mean, not humans. They had humans attached to them, hanging on to handles and being dragged along behind like men being taken out for a walk by dogs.

One of them looked familiar, but it wasn't until he spoke that I realized he was the cook that fries potatoes. 'How d'you turn this thing off, Leroy?' he whined.

Leroy's nice lazy voice answered from inside a pile of chairs in the middle of the room. 'Flick op de switch, man.'

Well, I thought, food at last, so I dodged through the chairs at once to find him. No food though. Only one of those thick fire-sticks of his, one of the sweet-smelling ones. He was lying on his back on a table in the middle of the pile with his eyes shut and the fire-stick between his fingers, smiling to himself. But he knew I was there even though he didn't open his eyes. 'Hi dere Cat,' he said and tickled me round the ears.

I was just estimating whether or not to jump up and sleep on his chest when He came roaring into the room. 'That carpet not up yet? What are you all playing at? What's that smell?' He'd picked up the scent of Leroy's fire-stick.

'That's the machine sir,' the potato boy said looking much too innocent to deceive anybody.

But He was deceived of course. 'Where's Leroy?'

'Gone to ring the decorators.'

'They should have been here two hours ago. The men from the council are here already. I want that carpet up and out before they start to fumigate.'

'Leave it to us, sir,' the potato boy said.

He gave his grunting 'All right then' noise and I thought we were going to get rid of him. But then he saw me. 'And what's that damn cat doing in here, for crying out loud? Get him out. She'll go spare if they fumigate *him*.'

Poor fool! Does he really imagine I'd let anyone fumigate me, whatever it is. I walked off towards the kitchen door at once, just to show him. And one of the boiler-suited men came out. He was wearing a white mask over his face and a white hood on his head and I must say he looked most peculiar. But there you are, there's no accounting for taste. Human beings love dressing up. They're always putting on odd clothes. I can't think why. They look uncouth whatever they wear.

The eyes between the hood and the mask were staring at me. 'That's a cat!' a voice said thickly through the white material. Brilliant! He can recognise a cat at three paces.

'It's going!' He said at once. 'Kevin's taking it upstairs, aren't you Kevin.'

No, he's not, I thought, and I made a sudden dart between his long legs and escaped into the corridor while they were all grabbing at the air where I'd been. From there it was two bounces into the street because the front door was ajar and the passage comfortable clear.

Once I was outside I stopped running at once and

walked away with my tail in the air to show them what fools they were being, but I was outside Leamington Spa's house before I stopped feeling cross.

I hadn't been back to Leamington Spa's since the night of the fire, so as I was there anyway I thought I might as well step in and see how she was, and whether she'd got anything for me to eat. The door was shut of course, but it wasn't long before it opened, and a sharp pair of high-heeled shoes came spiking out.

Leamington Spa's door was still lying on its side in the hall. So I got into her room straight away. I barely recognised the place. For a start it was absolutely filthy. Full of black slime, all over the floor and up the wall and smeared across the heat machine. And they've taken away her nice red chair and left a vile black one in its place covered in tar. I'm not surprised she hasn't come back. The bed was still in the corner and so was the table but all the saucepans were gone and there wasn't even the sniff of any food. In fact the smell of the place was the worst thing about it. Charred wood usually smells quite pleasant, prickly, of course, but not alarming. This smell was more than just charred wood. It was dirty and damp, a cross between mildew and used dishcloths and wet dust. Made me sneeze. No point staying in there, I can tell you.

By this time I was feeling decidedly hungry and as there didn't seem to be any human being around capable of providing me with sustenance, there was nothing for it but to hunt some down for myself. There's a scrubby little green just along the street where there are usually pigeons and sparrows and starlings strutting about. So I went there and caught myself a sparrow. Rather a scraggy one. Not much flesh on the bones, but better than nothing.

Then I went home.

Now after all the time I'd given them you really would have thought they'd have got the place back into some sort of order for me. I'd stayed out half the day. But no! It was worse than ever and it smelt absolutely revolting, a stinging, unnatural, oily sort of smell that clung inside your head. The carpet in the eating room had gone and so had the curtains and there were two men in overalls ripping the paper off the wall. I told you he'd gone mad, didn't I. And worse still the kitchen door wouldn't open, no matter what I did. I went upstairs to Jenny's room feeling very annoyed.

She'd come home while I was out. Wasn't that nice. She was lying in the bed making that funny barking-coughing noise, like they do sometimes. She was really pleased to see me, patting the coverlet and calling me up to join her. 'Hello my darling. Your poor old Mummy feels rotten. Come and keep me company.'

So I did, of course. It was splendidly warm up there on the duvet. We slept for most of the afternoon. It was quite dark when I woke up, and He was standing beside the bed with a tray full of food.

'Any better?' he said, switching on the bedside light.

'Not much,' she said. 'Are there any aspirin?'

He took a little white box out of his shirt pocket and rattled it at her. 'Aspirin, hot lemon, egg sandwiches, petit beurre,' he said. 'I see you've got company.'

'Let him stay,' she said, stroking my head. 'He's ever so good.'

'Ah, but does he feed you?'

'You're ever so good too. Especially today with the fumigation and everything.'

'All part of the service, ma'am,' and he bent down and pushed the damp hair off her forehead and kissed her. Then, wonder of wonders, he patted me on the head. Extraordinary! Perhaps that dreadful stink has done something to his brain.

So here we are, all nice and cosy in the duvet, dozing and purring and very very warm. Long may it continue.

Jenny and me have been sleeping for four days. And He's been really quite well-behaved, coming upstairs to see how we are and providing us with trays full of food, which she's picked at, and I've finished off for her. This is the life.

Or perhaps I should say, that was the life, because she got up this morning, I can't think why, and now she's groaning round the bedroom, wrapping herself up in layers and layers of wool, jerseys and legwarmers and a skirt like a blanket, so it looks as though she's going out. More's the pity. I've been sitting here in the bed watching her and making my pretty face so as to encourage her to change her mind. No good though. Human beings are very stubborn.

And now He's crashing up the stairs and putting that long nose round the bedroom door. 'Susie's here. You ready?'

'As I'll ever be. Where's the tissues?'

'Get that damn cat off the bed. We don't want fleas in the duvet. Off you!'

You see how cruel and unpredictable He is. Yesterday it was 'Nice to have a cat to keep you company!' Now it's 'Off you!'

'Oh don't throw him about like that,' she says. 'You know how he hates it. Look at his poor little face.'

'I haven't got time for his poor little face. Not today.'

I decided to go downstairs. The kitchen might be empty and the eating room full of machines but anything's better than being flung off the bed while they shout at each other.

Well, well, well. They've come to their senses downstairs I see. At last. The kitchen's full of people carrying in boxes and preparing food and rushing about just the same as usual. No bouncing machines as far as I can see and a heavenly smell of raw meat. I shall find Leroy and see what's on offer.

*

And very nice too, although I've had to wait for it most of the morning. Off cuts of beef, slithers of salmon, whitebait, a jar with the remains of some tarasamalata to lick clean. What I would call sensible eating.

Now for a rest. I wonder what the eating room's like.

Much improved. The carpet's back and the curtains and, what's even better, they've put a long table beside the wall, just where the floor is always warm, and they've covered it with a white cloth that reaches right down to the ground. It makes a first rate nest. I can have a really peaceful snooze here because no one will know where I am. I'll just settle myself into a really comfy position, tail curled round nose I think, that's always conducive to sleep. My whiskers this carpet's warm.

A fat lot of good that was. They were crashing in and out of the room all afternoon, like a herd of elephants with hob-nailed boots on, puffing and blowing and banging things down on the table right over my head, if you please, and kicking the tablecloth with their great feet right next to my tail, and making a noise machine blare right next to my ears. I have very acute hearing. I told you that didn't I. Not that I brag. It's a fact of feline life, that's all. But you can imagine how painful incessant banging is to a creature of such delicately adjusted senses. In the end I couldn't stand any more of it. I got up, had a good stretch, and walked out from underneath the tablecloth to shout at them.

They'd made some changes while I was under the table. The place was transformed. For a start, someone had brought a garden into the room. There were flowers everywhere, great big pink and white and yellow flowers that smelt of pepper. Rather overpowering. And glass everywhere too, hanging on the wall, glimmering like water, and sparkling on the tables, which were all in place and set with white cloths and eating sticks and little pink candles all alight and pink napkins folded like fans. The light was pretty poor though despite all those candles. No wonder they'd all been crashing about. I don't suppose they'd been able to see what they were doing. Human beings have very poor eyesight at the best of times, and even *I* was having a job to adjust to all those candles.

He was over by the door doing his oily act of ushering in half a dozen of those Yuppie people, who were all going 'Yah! Yah! Yah!' and looking at one another for approval. The female Yuppies flick their manes with their fingers and say 'OK Yah!' and the males snort and caper and say 'Yah! Yah! Start popping the poo, Piers.' They all have enormous feet and don't pay the slightest attention to where they're putting them, so I decided I'd keep well out of their way until He'd got them sitting on chairs. There were three waitresses hovering but I knew they wouldn't tread on me. I eased myself into the middle of the room. There was a big table there where I could hide if I needed to.

It was a very big table and piled high with fruit and flowers. More garden, you see. Smelt very strong. Very strong indeed. But when I got closer to it and away from the waxy smell of the candles I could detect all sorts of other scents too, roast beef, white fish, prawns, pork, some kind of bird flesh. And then I saw something quite amazing. There was a bird standing on the table, a live bird, perched right at the top of the pile, a huge bird with a great tail spread out like a fan. I could hardly believe my luck. It was standing very still, of course, and no wonder or it would have lost its balance. He'll get a shock when it flies off, I thought. Serve him right for bringing a garden into the house. It was almost as if it had gone into a 'freeze' like a hedgehog. Perhaps birds do that. Now birds are quite hard to catch out in the open. They strut about right in front of you, tormenting you, and then fly off just when you're ready to spring. But indoors they're much easier. For a start they can't fly far, and when they do, they exhaust themselves knocking into furniture. This one wouldn't get far. I could tell that just by looking at it. And looking at it was making my tail twitch. What a catch it would be. I could live off a bird like that for days and days. It occurred to me that I could creep up on it, because it was keeping absolutely still. Birds do that when they're alarmed too. So I slid up on it. Very slowly, creeping inch by inch, sliding and waiting, and sliding and waiting.

And waiting. And waiting...

When I pounced I was right on target. A quick nip to the neck and it was dead at once. Oh I'm a superlative hunter. Then all I had to so was to drag it off past the fruit, apples rolling and feathers flying. There was no weight to it at all for such a big bird.

I'd dragged it to the door before He started shouting. Stupid creature! Does he really imagine he can stop me? I pounded off down the corridor at full stride towards the back door. But some fool had shut it, and I could hear him running down the corridor after me. Quick, quick, quick. Find an open window.

There was one above the sink so I jumped up at once, dragged the carcass with me, but somehow or other I must have got the tail caught up on something because it ripped off, rustling like paper, and fell back onto the kitchen floor. Not that it mattered, because there's never much flesh on a tail. By this time I had my head through the window. Then my paws, tugging the neck between them. I was almost through, but the bird had got a lot heavier. It was really quite hard work lugging it about. Big body, small crack, that was the trouble. I tugged at it again. And suddenly the neck gave way and I was falling. I landed feet first of course, we cats always do, and the head and neck were still in my mouth. But instead of flesh there were great lumps of evil-smelling white stuff falling out of the neck. No meat. Just evil-smelling, inedible white stuff. I looked up and there was no flesh in the carcase either. Just the same horrible white stuff. It was a fraud! A sell! Oh how dishonest human beings are! Then I saw Him, grimacing behind the carcase, swearing and shouting, 'Damn cat!' Time to scarper.

I ran straight up the wall vertically and onto the roof of the outhouse, where I crouched down, perfectly still. I could hear him crashing about in the yard, flinging cardboard boxes right up in the air. 'He must be somewhere, God damn it. I'll kill him!' But I knew he wouldn't see me on the roof. He's far too short-sighted. Stupid creature.

'He gone over de wall man,' Leroy's voice said calmly.

'Four more customers, sir,' another voice said,

'What?' He said. 'Oh all right.'

Feet crashed back into the house.

It was jolly cold up there in the roof but I knew there must be a window open somewhere. There was a whole row of them just above me and one of them was showing a light. It was worth a try and safer than climbing down into the yard. So I climbed up.

And just as I'd climbed to the top of the roof I saw somebody standing right by the middle window, pulling her curtains and looking very neat and pale in her working black dress. It was Jenny. I called to her at once so that she'd open the window and let me in.

But she didn't. She'd seen me. I could tell by the affectionate expression on her face. And she'd got her hand on the catch ready to open the window and I was waiting below her, all wide-eyed and hopeful just on the other side of the glass, when his horrible voice roared out right behind her.

'Is that damn cat in here?'

It made her jump. She pulled the curtains shut and turned to face him. 'No. You can see he isn't.'

'Damn thing! I'll kill him when I catch him.'

'What's the poor thing supposed to have done now?'

'Only ruined my centrepiece, that's all. Run off with the peacock. Right in front of everybody.'

'Oh dear,' she said, But she wasn't cross. I could tell. Her voice was bubbly, the way it always is just before she starts to laugh. 'Oh dear. Was anybody there?'

'Half a dozen Yuppies. They thought it was funny.'

'Well so it is.' She was laughing out loud. 'Very funny! Oh come on, it *was* a bird after all and he's a hunter. You might have known something like this would happen.'

'Oh that's right! Take his side, I should. After all I'm only the owner of this restaurant and he's a *cat*.'

Well, well, I thought, He's understood the situation at last. Brilliant!

'You wait till I catch him. I'll give him such a thrashing he'll never run off with anything else for the rest of his life. If he lives.'

What? What? He can't mean that surely, I thought. Not now he's understood how important I am. He's got to be joking. There was a crack in the curtains so I peered through to see for myself. But no, he'd got a really foul look on his face. She was undoing the buttons of her black dress.

'Now what are you doing?' he said, scowling at her.

'You can see what I'm doing,' she said calmly. 'I'm changing.'

His face was a study. Furious and baffled. 'You can't do that,' he said. 'Not tonight. You promised to help me. Remember? You can't go back on your promise. Not tonight.' What a whingeing voice he's got!

She turned right round in her chair to look at him. 'When I said I'd come and live here with you, you gave me a promise too. You promised to take my cat and give him a good home and look after him just the same as I would. Now you're threatening to kill him. I'd call that going back on a promise, wouldn't you?'

'I wouldn't kill him. You know that.'

'Do I? You're always saying you'll hit him.'

'I haven't though, have I?'

'You just might. You're a terrible bully.'

That's it, I thought. You tell him.

'I haven't got time for all this,' He said crossly. 'Are you going to help me or aren't you?'

'Are you going to hit my cat or aren't you?'

'Oh come on, for Pete's sake, it's not important.'

'It is to me.'

There was a long pause, while they looked at one another. He was staring her out, trying to bully her into agreeing with him. But she didn't give way. She went on staring and in the end he was the one who dropped his eyes and admitted defeat. Well good for you, I thought. It's about time you beat him.

'OK. OK. Have it your own way,' he said. 'You win. He'll be the most spoilt objectionable creature, but if that's what you want. Just come down and help, that's all. Please.'

'I'll be down in two minutes.'

He almost smiled at her, standing at the door. Oh go away, do! I thought. I was freezing to death out there on the roof.

And at long, long last he went. Thank heavens for that.

'You bad cat,' she said to me as she opened the window. But then she picked me and cuddled me underneath her chin and stroked me and kissed the top of my head. 'Fancy nicking his peacock! His prize peacock. Oh dear, oh dear!' She put me on the sofa in their living room. 'You stay there and keep out of mischief. I'll feed you when I get back.'

She won't of course. She always forgets when she's been down in that restaurant all evening. Still never mind. At least it's warm in here. And at least she's told him a thing or two.

I shall sleep on his sweater. That's what I'll do. And I hope he gets fleas.

CHAPTER 5

Leroy and I are making a new room for poor old Leamington Spa. What do you think of that? We're doing it out of the kindness of our hearts because we're both rather noble creatures. Not that I brag. Nobility like ours is inborn. You've either got it or you haven't.

Some of his friends come and help us from time to time. There were six of them yesterday. It was quite a crush. But we are bearing the brunt of it. Leroy says so. 'Dis cat an' dis boy yere bearin' de brunt,' he says. He always calls himself 'dis boy yere'. I think that's nice. Sounds right.

We spend as much time at Leamington Spa's as we can. We go down in the morning, when He's 'taken delivery', which means carrying boxes and cartons and things like that into the kitchen, and shouting 'Mind your backs!' and glaring at me. Then Leroy and I trot off down the road and work very, very hard until it's time to go back to start the lunches. He paints doors and window-sills and hangs wallpaper and scrubs out cupboards, and I sit on the table and supervise, which is very important. Leroy says so. 'Couldn't get de work done widout Cat,' he says. Which is perfectly true. I admit it.

Yesterday he put a new heat machine into the wall. I think it's called 'the insurance' because Leroy said we could get on, 'now we got the insurance.' It's a splendid machine and gives out much more warmth than the old one, and lights with just a little soft 'plop', which is a marked improvement too. The only trouble is that Leroy won't always light it. He had it glowing beautifully for a very short time yesterday so that I could sit in front of it, but then he turned it off, and he hasn't lit it again although I've thrown out all the hints I could think of, sitting in front of it and staring at it, and walking up and down where the hearth rug used to be. It's not like Leroy to be so unobservant. Still I suppose it's because he's so busy.

Today we are finishing the wallpaper, which is really quite pretty, all pink and blue flowers and green leaves. Black cats would have been better, of course, and looked a great deal more stylish, but flowers are the next best thing. Leroy cuts it up and pastes it and spreads it on the wall with a big brush, and I sit on the table and guard the rolls.

'Wha' you tink Cat?' Leroy says. 'Neat eh? We don't tell she what we doin'. We give she surprise.'

I look hopefully at the heat machine but he still doesn't notice. It's none too warm in here. The wind blows straight up the hall whenever anyone opens the front door. I ruffle my fur and look at the heat machine again. Still no response. Perhaps I'll try sneezing.

*

It's getting colder and colder. Last night it rained ice. Imagine that! When I came in from the yard my fur was spiked with it. Not at all pleasant, I can tell you. Jenny was very concerned and let me jump up into her lap at once and get warm. Oh she's a lovely creature sometimes. He said I was leaving damp patches on the carpet, which was *not* true. Cats never leave damp patches anywhere. It's not in our nature. We're not dogs! Luckily she didn't take any notice of him. She got a towel and rubbed me dry and told me I was her darling and the best of cats, which I knew anyway but it's nice to hear it said. Then we sat on the sofa, all curled up together, while He crashed about downstairs below us.

I was actually quite glad to be inside in the warm, and it wasn't just because I was out in the rain either. Something rather odd has been going on outside for the last few days. As soon as it begins to get dark in the middle of the afternoon, things start going bang. Sometimes it's just one sharp crack, which makes you jump but is soon over, but sometimes it's a whole series of explosions that go on and on. If you look up you can see sparks in the sky and smell a sharp prickly scent which is rather alarming. I'm not afraid of it, you understand. We cats are creature of immense courage. But it's more comfortable indoors.

Perhaps I'll stay in the house tomorrow. I daresay Leroy could get along without me to help him. He seems to know what he's doing now. And besides I ought to keep her company.

*

Well we've had two very pleasant days in the warm together. The rain was streaming down the windows all the time, so we stayed indoors. For a human being Jenny's very sensible. And they had kippers for breakfast today and as He invariably leaves half of his, wasteful creature, there was plenty for me to eat.

But now she's gone rushing off to that school place again. I've had a nice long snooze on her duvet and I've finished off the milk she put down for me and had a lick and a promise and now I think I'll stroll down and see what Leroy's doing.

Cooking whitebait and not giving any to me, and singing at the top of his voice. Really the noise in this kitchen is unbearable. And if nobody's going to feed me, I'm off. I'll shout at the door to the yard. They always let me out at once when I do that.

I shan't stay in the yard though. It's been the most uninteresting place since He had his fumigation. All the dustbins are so tightly sealed you can't even smell anything through them, leave alone drag it out, and there's nothing else there at all now, except empty cardboard boxes all stacked together against the wall. Useless.

I'll run along the wall and jump down into the big garden at the end of the row. There are mice in there sometimes, and quite tasty ones too. Or failing that a vole or a frog. You never know what scent you'll pick up till you start.

I've had the most dreadful experience.

I found the garden all right and jumped down into the laurel bush which usually gives me pretty good cover whenever I hunt there. But the moment my forepaws touched the earth everything exploded. I know you'll find that hard to believe but that is truly what happened. Everything exploded. Everything! There were hideous crashing sounds all round me and the most dreadful wailings and whizzings rushing straight up into the air. I was being attacked from all sides. It was absolutely fiendish. My fur was standing on end so much I could the cold air blowing straight onto my flesh. I wonder my heart didn't stop beating.

I stood my ground under the laurel and put up a fight, of course, because no cat is a coward. I swore and spat and bared my teeth and put my ears back as far as they would go. But that didn't stop anything. The explosions went on and on and so did the terrible dazzling lights and the wailing and all those invisible things rushing through the air. And then there were three dark figures just in front of me waving white fire about, round and round, and dropping hot sparks in every direction.

In the end I just put my head back and howled. I couldn't help it. On and on. "Aow! Aow! Aow!" and presently I could feel the vibrations of human feet approaching across the grass and a face peered down into the bush at me and a voice said,' Hang on a minute Gerry. There's a cat in here.' And the explosions stopped.

I went on growling, of course, because no cat with his wits about him ever stops fighting until he's sure, but I was listening and watching too, and they *had* stopped and so had the flashing lights. The three dark shapes rolled towards me out of the darkness and became children wrapped in duffle coats and woolly hats and scarves. But the devils were still about. There was a terrible smell of fire and sulphur.

'Kitty-kitty-kitty,' one of the children called. 'Here kitty-kitty-kitty.'

I retreated into the bush, swearing. And my heels touched the brick wall. It gave me a terrifying sensation that I was being hemmed in. I knew at once that if I didn't make a supreme effort I would be caught and exploded too.

I pulled my wits and my energies into the strongest force I could muster and jumped through the hedge onto the lawn, and ran and ran at full stretch until I was out in the road on the other side of the house. There was a long line of dark cars standing beside the pavement. I was safe underneath the nearest one the moment I saw it, I don't mind telling you. What luck!

I stayed there keeping very still and quiet until I'd got my breath back. The explosions were going on all the time. But they couldn't get at me, of course. Not in my hiding place. We cats always chose the most excellent hiding places. Not that I brag. It's our superior intelligence, that's all.

The only trouble was there was something black and oily dripping out of the car and some of it fell on my back, which was most unpleasant, so I knew I couldn't stay there for very long, explosions or no explosions. I waited until there was a lull and then I ran out between the front wheels and along the gutter, keeping my belly very close to the ground, until I was underneath the next car along. It was easy. Well I knew it would be. For a cat of my speed and intelligence anything was possible. Even on a night when everything's exploding.

The oil was a problem though. I tried twitching my coat but that was no good at all. Didn't dislodge a single drop of the filthy stuff and made me acutely aware of how cloying and disagreeable it was. I knew I ought to sit up and give my fur a thorough grooming but you can't sit up when you're underneath a car. It's absolutely revolting under there. If you so much as brushed your coat against the underside you'd be covered in greasy dust. Human beings are horribly dirty creatures. They only clean the parts that show. It's something I've frequently noticed. He spends hours polishing the top of his car but I've never seen him wash underneath the thing. No, there was nothing for it, I would have to go home, somehow or other, and get cleaned up. But how? I sat under the second car and gave the matter thought.

Running straight home in the open was out of the question of course, because it would mean passing the garden where the worst of the explosions were.

Following the pavement wouldn't be much better either, because there were explosions coming from every direction now, and no way of knowing where or when the next barrage would begin. No, there was only one thing to be done, and that was to keep under cover and run from car to car following the road. I could head off in the right direction when there was a turning.

It was a terrifying journey. I persevered, of course, because I'm an animal of quite outstanding courage, but many a lesser creature would have given up, I can tell you. Especially when the distance between one car and the next was more than two explosions long. As it was on far too many runs.

But there *was* a side road, just as I'd foreseen, and there were cars parked the full length of it and on my side of the road too, which was a bit of luck. So eventually, after running for ever, I arrived in my own street. Just outside old Leamington Spa's to be exact, and who should be strolling along the pavement just ahead of me but Leroy. I could see him quite clearly in the light of the nearest street lamp. Walking along with his friends in that easy rolling way of his as if he wasn't afraid of anything. I put on a spurt and caught up with him, running between his feet as he walked so that he couldn't help noticing me.

'What you doin' out here on Guy Fawkes night?' he said, bending down to stroke me. 'You crazy or somethin'?'

'Dat de ol' woman' cat, ain' he?' another man said,

squinting down at me.

'No he ain',' Leroy said, but I couldn't hear what he said next, because there were two absolutely enormous explosions right overhead. They were so loud they made me shake. Not through fear you understand. No, no. It was just the volume of sound that was all. But Leroy couldn't bear to see me upset, no matter what the reason, because he's got a tender heart, so he bent down at once and scooped me up in one hand and put me inside his jacket and that made the explosions stop. Then we all went jogging off along the road to the restaurant, which wasn't as unpleasant as you might think, because Leroy runs in the same way as he walks, in a nice easy swaying rhythm, so being carried in his jacket was like swinging in a hammock, and that's something a cat can endure fairly equitably, providing it doesn't got on for too long.

We were back in the kitchen before the explosions began again. Leroy lifted me out of his jacket and set me down on the floor. I started to wash my back immediately, and it was very difficult and evil-tasting, I can tell you. Leroy watched me for a few moments, then he looked at the palms of his hands and grimaced. 'What you got on your coat, Cat?' he said. 'You cover me in grease.'

'That's sump oil, Leroy,' the potato boy said. 'He's been under a car.'

'He smother',' Leroy said. 'Go get de meffs, Tony. We clean he.'

Somebody produced a bottle of mauve liquid and a roll of cotton wool and Leroy lifted me up again and stood me on the workbench on a sheet of newspaper, which was rather undignified, but I allowed it because I knew he wouldn't do anything to hurt me. And besides it was proving quite horribly difficult to remove that oil, so if he intended to help me perhaps it was a good thing. But the smell of that meffs! Very unpleasant.

Leroy and the potato boy cleaned my coat between them. You should have seen the muck that came off it onto that cotton wool. Dark brown filth, pads and pads of it. What a relief when it was all gone! I felt like a new cat.

As soon as they'd finished rubbing me with cotton wool, they let me jump down and clean myself properly, while they went back to their cooking. Very sensible. And as there was no sign of Him and everybody seemed to be in a cheerful mood I decided to stay where I was and have a short nap. Excitement is all very well but it's very exhausting.

But I'd hardly been asleep for more than a minute or two when somebody lifted me out of my basket and dangled me in the air. 'We taking the cat, Leroy?' a voice said, right beside my ear and very loudly.

No, I thought to myself, you are *not*. Don't you even think it. And I made my disapproving face, ears right back and snarl beginning.

'You frighten he,' Leroy's voice said from somewhere behind me, and then his brown hands reached into the line of vision and supported me under the back legs and lifted me out of trouble. Not a moment too soon, or I would have clawed that other fool's hands. I narrowed my eyes at him and gave him my loving look, but do you know I don't think he even noticed. He put me straight inside his jacket again, and he was talking all the time. 'You got de cover' dish, Gerry? No, no, de big one. Taters. Sparagus. Soufflé. Right. Right.'

Then he opened the door and the boy called Gerry pushed the food trolley down the corridor. But to my utter astonishment he walked right past the eating room and out into the street. And Leroy and the potato boy followed him. With explosions going on all round us, and the weather perfectly abysmal, and absolutely every reason for staying indoors. There are times when I really do wonder whether *any* human being is intelligent. I shouted at Leroy to let him know what I thought about such folly but he only stroked me under the chin and held me firmly with one hand and said, 'Soon be dere Cat.' Soon be where? That's what I'd like to know.

We all went jogging back down the street towards Leamington Spa's, and it was colder than ever, but at least there weren't any more explosions, which was something to be thankful for I suppose. And just as we reached the gate to her dusty old garden, two other men came up to us, nodding and talking and breathing plumes of steam out of their mouths.

'You got the cat I see,' one said, poking me, very

unnecessarily, with a gloved finger.

And the other one said, 'Let's go!' and led the way into Leamington Spa's house. What an extraordinary thing! We all went trooping in after him, Poking Finger, me and Leroy, Gerry and the potato boy and the trolley and everything, down the hall and through the new door and right into the room.

And there was Leamington Spa herself, sitting in a new armchair next to her new heat machine with a new rug over her legs. Well, well, well. I was so surprised I could feel my eyes bolting.

'Dinner is serve ma'am,' Leroy said. And he put me down on the hearthrug next to the heat machine, and he and Gerry bustled about and unpacked a tray which they fitted across Leamington Spa's legs, with a little cloth to cover it, and a red flower in a little vase and then an entire steaming meal on a very hot plate. Roast chicken and bacon rolls. Delicious. Enough to make anybody's whiskers twitch. Leamington Spa's fairly stood on end.

'Oh how kind!' she said. 'How very kind.'

'Compliments a' Peacock Pie,' Leroy said, beaming at her. 'Eat it all up. Don' you let it go col', when I cook it for you.'

'And chicken too,' Leamington Spa said to the two strange men. 'Isn't that kind. My favourite.'

'One picture of you and your cat,' Poking Finger said, 'before you settle down to your meal. Could you get him to sit on your lap?'

'He's not really my cat,' Leamington Spa said,

smiling at me. 'I have half-shares you might say. But I daresay he would sit on my lap if I were to offer him some of this excellent chicken. Is that all right Leroy?'

'It your chicken,' Leroy said.

'Then in that case,' Leamington Spa said, 'we'll share it, shall we Cat?'

Oh what an excellent creature she is. I'm so glad she's come back home. Even if fools like Poking Finger point one of their wretched boxes at you and flash lights out of it just when you're in the middle of the first mouthful of good food you've tasted for nearly twenty-four hours.

CHAPTER 6

Leroy has turned traitor! Imagine that! Yes, I know I told you how splendid he was, and until this morning he was, the nearest thing to a cat on human legs. Which makes his present behaviour all the more reprehensible. If I hadn't seen it with my own sharp eyes I wouldn't have believed it. And I do have exceptionally good eyesight, I told you that didn't I? Oh I'm so upset it's taken away my appetite.

I came down to the kitchen this morning at my usual time and was let in as usual and breakfast was quite palatable, even though it took the new boy far too long to remember to put it down for me. I had to shout at him for ages before he did as he was told. I was cleaning my whiskers, when I heard the door swing open and Leroy's nice easy smell came drifting into the room before him. I looked up, of course, ready to greet him, because he likes a greeting first thing in the morning, and I simply couldn't believe what I saw.

He was standing right in front of me, wearing his nice smelly jeans and that fur-edged jacket, and just below his chin was another cat. A horrible scrawny little thing! In *my* kitchen! I was so angry I almost stopped breathing. Then I swore, of course, and put my back up and made my fur stand on end so that neither of them could have the slightest doubt how I felt about being invaded. And Leroy laughed! Laughed! Imagine that! And I always thought he was such a fine man.

And then, as if that wasn't bad enough, he went off to the milk cupboard and got *two* saucers and poured milk into both of them and set them down on the floor at opposite ends of the kitchen, with that foul little cat smirking inside his jacket all the time. 'Come on Cat,' he said, looking straight at me. 'Come an' get it.'

Come and get it! Is that any way to speak to a cat of my calibre, I ask you. Well if he thinks I'm going to demean myself by eating in the same kitchen as a common little upstart, he's got another think coming. I won't. And that's all there is to that. I'll sit by the saucer, just to make sure the upstart doesn't take liberties with what's mine, but I won't drink it.

They're all behaving in the most ridiculous way. You'd think they'd never seen a small cat before. I know they're used to my magnificence, but it's nothing to look at, all long straggly legs and thin spine, and tabby, of course. So common. But they've all been clustering round it watching it eat and making stupid noises at it. You know the sort of thing. Oooh! Aaagh! Gaa-gaa! Infantile sort of stuff. And now the potato boy is running about with a cardboard box making a nest for it, if you ever heard of anything so silly. Surely they don't want to encourage it. If they go on like this, it'll stay here, and they won't like that.

And now what do you think they've done? They've put their stupid cardboard box right next to the second oven. In the exact spot where I always sit when the east wind blows. I can't think what the world is coming to. Have they no sense of priority? They all *know* that's my place. Nobody else has any right to it. And certainly not another cat. It's lying there all comfortably curled up as if it owns the place. The effrontery of it! You just wait till the coast is clear and they've gone off home for the afternoon, I'll send it packing with two snarls. And Leroy needn't think I'll pay any attention to *him* today. Not after this. I shall sit with my back to him and I hope it hurts his feelings.

They went on playing with the kitten for *hours* after they'd finished the lunch. I thought they were never going home. And it slept all the time, with its paws over its nose, not even looking at them. In the end they got fed-up with it and began to drift off through the swing doors, clump, clump, one after the other. And about time too.

Leroy was the last to go and he came over to tickle me under the chin to say goodbye the way he usually does. I sat quite still, bolt upright of course, to show how cross I was and gave him my reproachful stare. And he grinned as if it was all a great joke. 'Look after Kitty,' he said. 'Treat she good.'

Oh, I'll treat she good. You just watch me.

I walked over to the second oven the minute the kitchen was clear, and growled at her. But she didn't wake up. She didn't even stir. She went on sleeping with her paws over her nose. It was rather demoralising I can tell you. So I tried dabbing at her. With one paw and barely any claws at all. Just enough to warn her off and show her she wasn't wanted. But she ignored that too. She twitched her ears once or twice, but she still didn't wake up. How stupid and insensitive can you get?

In the end I decided to leave her where she was and go and have my siesta. It's very warm in the kitchen when all the ovens have been on and I'd made a pretty good meal, when Leroy wasn't looking, so I needed a rest, for the sake of my digestive system if nothing else. I could chastise the upstart later on. It was simply a matter of choosing the right moment that was all.

Well I've had a nice long nap and I've woken feeling quite refreshed. This kitchen is a good place for napping, providing you do it before they all come back and start crashing about again. A steady warmth is conducive to sleep and so is being stroked or groomed. There's someone cleaning my back at the moment. The rhythm is excellent and, whoever it is, is being very thorough. It's almost like being cleaned by another cat. Very satisfactory. I shall lie here and enjoy it for a little longer and then I'll open my eyes and see who it is. Ummm! Yes!

You're never going to believe this. It's the upstart. Can you imagine that? She was still hard at it when I opened my eyes. I was so surprised it made me blink. But there you are. There's some sense in her after all. Knows her place, that's what it is. I must say I find that rather impressive. I didn't think she'd turn out to be a sensible cat. When I've had a good stretch I shall give her a bit of a wash too. From the look of it she doesn't seem to be able to reach the end of her tail – no fault of hers, she's young - and a bit of mutual grooming never goes amiss. Then I'll take her out in the yard and show her the best places for a spot of sunbathing, providing it doesn't rain.

The yuppies are back. The eating room is full of them all barking and baying in those loud voices of theirs and moving the chairs about, which is so unnecessary. When me and Kitty arrived, poor old Leamington Spa was sitting all squashed up in a corner and she only had one other chair at her table. I jumped up and sat in it at once before they could move *that*. You have to be firm when you're dealing with Yuppies.

Leamington Spa gave me one of her nice smiles. 'Hello Cat,' she said. 'Who's your friend?'

Kitty was sitting on the floor where I'd left her, looking up at us, sort of hopefully, and there was a huge pair of feet just behind her, heading straight towards her. The potato boy. Wouldn't you know it?

'Mind the little cat,' Leamington Spa said, smiling at him.

'That's Kitty,' he told her. 'Issen she a cutie? We been playing with her all morning.'

'She'll get trampled on if she sits down there,' Leamington Spa said. 'I've never seen the place so crowded. Could you pick her up, do you think, and put her on the chair next to my Cat? She'll be safe with him, won't she Cat.'

I gave her my loving smile to show her how intelligent she was being and while I was doing it the potato boy picked Kitty up by the scruff of her neck and dumped her down beside me. She looked a bit surprised, poor little thing, so I narrowed my eyes and gave him my disapproving look. He doesn't have to be so rough with her. She's only a kitten.

'Now then,' he said, taking his pencil from behind his ear. 'Roast of the day was it?'

I was really quite relieved when he walked away. He's such an oaf.

'Now I've got two cats to keep me company,' Leamington Spa said, smiling at me. 'I can't think of anything nicer.'

I gave her my prettiest smile, naturally, because it's gratifying to be appreciated, but I was actually wondering how long it would be before the potato boy brought our food. I'll bet it takes him ages and it's tantalising to smell all the tasty things other people are poking into their mouths in that inelegant way of theirs when you're waiting forever for something to be brought to *your* table. Especially when you're starving. Of course, we cats are extremely patient.

Patience is part of our nature and I'm probably the most patient cat alive. But there are limits. Kitty's no good at it at all. She can't wait a second. She started clawing the tablecloth and trying to climb up onto the table as soon as the potato boy put her on the chair. I dabbed her with my paw to remind her how to behave but she took no notice and, in the end, she fell, just as I knew she would, backwards off the edge of the table onto the carpet. She made a good landing, I'll say that for her, but poor old Leamington Spa was really upset. And just as everybody was looking our way and laughing, a familiar hand passed right in front of my eyes. I'd have known whose hand it was even before I saw it because I recognised the excellent smell of it, horses, donkeys, cats, spearmint, cats' meat, compost. It was the cattery man.

He picked Kitty up very gently, a mother cat couldn't have done it better, and then lowered her gently onto the chair. 'I think this is yours ma'am,' he said to Leamington Spa.

'How kind,' Leamington Spa said, smiling at him. 'She's not very good at table manners yet, I'm afraid.'

Then he noticed me and stopped to tickle me behind the ears the way he used to do. 'Now this splendid creature is an old friend,' he said. 'How are you Cat?'

'He's a hero,' Leamington Spa said, leaning across the table towards us. 'If it hadn't been for him I would have died in a house fire. Imagine that. He raised the alarm just in time, so the firemen said.'

'That doesn't surprise me a bit,' the cattery man said, turning to make way for someone who'd come up behind him. 'I always said he was a splendid cat. What do you think of that Malc?'

It was another man, sort of sand coloured with a sand coloured beard, rather scruffy-looking and smelling of school. He was standing right in the path the waiters take between the tables so I flattened my ears and gave him one of my looks. I hope Leamington Spa doesn't encourage him or he'll hold up the food. 'Think of what?' he said.

'This cat is a hero. He saved this lady from a fire.'

Sandyman looked at me. 'Oh yes,' he said. 'I remember. Jenny told me. It was all in the papers. Caused quite a stir.' And he bent down and stroked my back, which was gratifying although of course richly deserved. 'Actually,' he said, looking at Leamington Spa, 'we came over to ask you a favour. We've been looking for a seat – well two seats really – and we couldn't see *one* when we first came in – is it always this crowded? - and we were wondering whether you might let us join you at your table.'

'Well...' Leamington Spa said doubtfully. 'I've only got the one spare seat, as you see, and that's rather taken at the moment. If you could find two more chairs...'

I could smell the food arriving, all meaty and steaming, so I looked hopefully at Leamington Spa to encourage her to stop talking but she wasn't looking at me. And then another voice joined in the conversation and it was Jenny, wearing that horrible black outfit and carrying a tray with a covered dish on it.

'Good heavens!' Malc said. 'Jenny! What *are* you doing? You're surely not working here?'

She looked annoyed and gave him her careful smile. 'I help out now and then,' she said. 'When there's a rush.' And she balanced the tray on the edge of the table, lifted the cover from the dish and put the plate right in front of Leamington Spa. It smelt wonderful. Made my mouth water. If the cattery man will just take the sandy man somewhere else, we can get down to some serious eating.

But he's still talking. 'We've had the most horrendous day at school,' he said to the cattery man. 'The kids were manic. I don't think either of us sat down from one end of the day to the other. I know I didn't. She should be getting a bit of a rest not running about waiting at table.'

I narrowed my eyes to show him he was overstepping the mark. I don't want to hear how horrendous the school was being. I want my food. But they went on talking. That's the trouble with humans. They will talk. It's so unnecessary.

'Needs must when the devil drives,' she said to him, shrugging her shoulders. Then she looked at Leamington Spa. 'Enjoy your meal, ma-am,' she said. 'Is there anything else you need?'

Leamington Spa smiled up at her. 'Well now,' she said. 'Would it be possible for you to rustle up two more chairs? I know it's a lot to ask but your friends haven't got anywhere to sit and there'd be room for them here, if you could find a couple of chairs for them.'

'I'll see what I can do,' she said.

No, no, no! I thought. We don't want you to do anything. We want to get on with our food. But it was no good. She went rushing off with her empty tray and the cattery man and the Sandyman stood around taking up space and Leamington Spa looked at her plate and didn't even begin to eat. It was too bad. I tried looking pathetic but none of them did anything.

So we all had to wait until Jenny came struggling back with two chairs from the bar and then they had to settle at the table – and that took for ever – and then she had to take their order which was another waste of time and poor old Leamington Spa went on looking longingly at her plate and waited. The meat was cold by the time we got to eat it. Still at least the cattery man came up trumps. He had salmon and gave us titbits until there was nothing more left on his plate. Sandyman, I need hardly say, was useless. All he wanted to do was talk about school and how hard Jenny worked and what a fine woman she was. He kept saying she was a giddy marvel and he didn't know how she coped with some of the kids.

'She shouldn't be working as a waitress,' he said to Leamington Spa. 'She should be taken out to dinner and waited on by someone else. What's up with that bloke of hers?'

Leamington Spa wiped her mouth with her napkin. 'He doesn't even know the right way to treat a cat,' she said, 'let alone a partner, or whatever it is she calls him.'

'That's rather what I thought,' the cattery man said. 'When they brought your hero to the cattery he was very rough with him. I couldn't say anything, naturally, but he was.'

'She's wasted on him,' Sandyman said. 'I've thought that for ages. Ever since she first took up with him.'

The cattery man gave him a warning look. 'Hush up!' he said. 'She's coming for the empty plates.'

And they *were* empty. There wasn't a scrap left for anyone. Even Kitty could see that. So we jumped down and went off to find a warm place for a snooze.

Well Kitty and I have had four very busy days. I've taken her round the yard and shown her all the best places to sleep and hide in and I've taken her to the big garden at the end of the row and shown her where to dig and I've led her all over the house, when He wasn't looking, and shown her the most comfortable beds and the easiest chairs to climb and we've had our supper with Leamington Spa every evening, when Sandyman wasn't getting in our way. He's a nice enough man. I'll say that for him. He knows how to recognise quality in a cat and treats us properly. But he's beginning to be a nuisance. The trouble is he comes in every evening to talk to Jenny, which I might say is extremely unnecessary, and then he stands in the gangway talking about school and what hard work it is and what a nightmare day they've both had and everything gets held up. He really ought to know better, when you think how hard I've been working and how much I need my food. It's a heavy responsibility bringing up a kitten. Not that I complain. I do it willingly because I'm a cat of very high principles, but he ought to be more considerate of my feelings. Still there you are. That's humans for you. I've said it before and I'll say it again. They *will* talk.

Kitty and me have been asleep on Jenny's bed all afternoon, curled up together in the warm. He's been crashing about in the kitchen, banging things and shouting so we're keeping out of the way. She came into the room a few minutes ago and told us what good cats we were, which we knew of course, but it's nice to be told, and now she's sitting in front of her mirror with a towel round her head spreading colours on her face with those funny sticks of hers, rubbing them over her mouth and poking at her eyes with them. Humans are very peculiar sometimes, even nice ones like her. But at least it's peaceful. Or it was until he came in. We heard his feet crashing up the stairs and now he's running round the room shouting. 'Aren't you ready? We open in five minutes.' Kitty was quite frightened until I put a paw on her. I've got a very good way with kittens. Not that I brag. It's a fact of feline life. Or my particular feline life. And I'm certainly not going to take any notice of someone roaring. He can roar all he likes. Although I must say he's going it at the moment.

'Oh come on, for Pete's sake,' he shouts. 'You don't need make-up to wait at table.'

'How many more times have I got to tell you?' she says, poking away at her eyes. 'It's the party. I'm going out.'

'Oh come on, Jen,' he says using his wheedling voice. 'You don't mean it. I mean you don't have to go, do you? Not tonight. We've got a full house. And George is worse than useless. Do it for me, eh?'

'You're wasting your breath,' she says, turning her head to look at him. 'I'm going. I've made my mind up.'

He snorts through that horrible nose of his. 'That's just typical of you,' he says. 'You're so selfish. What about the restaurant? How am I supposed to run it if you won't help me?'

'That,' she says, putting down her eye stick and unwinding the towel, 'is your problem. If I were on the staff it would be different. But I'm not am I?'

'I thought you loved me,' he says, putting on a silly face.

'So did I,' she says, brushing her hair. 'Now I'm beginning to wonder.'

He's looking at the machine on his wrist. 'Oh for crying out loud!' he shrieks. 'Three minutes! Get those dammed cats off the bed.' Then he bangs out of the door and crashes off down the stairs. I must say we're well rid of him. Damned cats indeed!

She picks up one of her machines and makes a breeze come out of it and holds it towards her head. Kitty's very surprised but of course I've seen it all before. It's what she always does when she's had a towel round her head. Then she puts on one of her pretty dresses, kisses us both and leaves us. Time to join Leamington Spa I think.

The eating room is full of very loud people and Leamington Spa is squashed in her corner again, but there's vacant seat for us right next to her, so we climb up and wait. It takes ages before there's any food in front of us and the waiters are all rushing about like maniacs, bumping into one another and spilling things. But at least Sandyman isn't here clogging up the gangway. And that's one good thing.

CHAPTER 7

I've said it before but I'll say it again. Human beings are weird. There's no other word for them. They don't know how to feed properly and they don't know how to wash themselves, and, what with their machines and their loud voices, they make ridiculous noises all the time and none of them have got the faintest idea how important it is to sit still and keep quiet. If they just took a few minutes now and then to watch our superlative example, they might learn something. But they don't. Take this evening.

I've just been down to the garden at the end of the row to do a little private digging and see if there was anything there worth hunting and I was kicking the earth back into place with my back paws in my usual neat way when I heard a very peculiar noise, not exactly shouting and not exactly singing but a sort of mixture. Naturally I was alerted so I climbed up on the fence at once to see what was going on. All cats are inquisitive. It's part of our nature and a very sensible part. And the street was full of people, all striding along together with their arms linked and their mouths open making noises and all of them dressed up in the most peculiar clothes. One was wearing a dinner plate on her head and a long scarf made of feathers, if you can believe such a thing, and another had a black patch over one eye and was waving a stick about and another one was carrying a ridiculous toy cat. They were all very jolly, no threat at all, so I watched from my perch on the fence to see where they were going and they went rollicking off along the road and turned in at the 'Peacock Pie'. Imagine that. Naturally I dodged back along the alley and trotted off at once to see what they were going to do next. It was nearly time for Leamington Spa to turn up for her dinner anyway and I was feeling hungry as well as curious.

Kitty was waiting for me half way down the stairs and as soon as she saw me she came lolloping down to join me and we walked into the eating room together with our tails held straight in the air. And what a crush there was. We could barely squeeze our way through.

He was shouting across the room. 'Look who's arrived, Jen. It's the Bluebells. Back for the pantomime.' There are times when I don't understand a word he's saying. What bluebells? I can't see any.

Jenny was standing beside a corner table talking to the Yuppies and writing in her little notebook but when she looked up and saw the newcomers she put her pencil in her pocket and walked over at once, smiling at them.

'Hi there!' she said. 'Table for twelve wasn't it?'

The man with the toy cat said, 'Thirteen actually. Is that all right? We won't bring you bad luck.'

He was smiling in that unctuous way of his. 'No problem,' he said. 'We're always ready to provide an extra chair, aren't we Jen. It'll be a bit of a squeeze but you won't mind that will you.'

I gave him my disapproving look. Now she'll have to start dragging chairs about. I can't see him doing it. But he didn't pay any attention.

'So what's the great opus this year?' he said, when they were getting seated and she'd gone off to get that dratted chair for them.

The one with the toy cat lifted it up in the air. 'Guess,' he said

'Puss in Boots?'

'Try again. Think Lord Mayor of London.'

'Dick Whittington. I say! That's ambitious.'

The woman smothered in feathers was looking at me. 'You've got a cat in here,' she said. 'Is it yours?'

He looked across at me. 'Oh yes,' he said. 'He's mine. He was Jen's originally but we sort of share him now. Let me know if he's a nuisance and I'll get rid of him.'

Leamington Spa was walking past the table, leaning on her stick. She scowled at him and leant across the table to talk to Feathers. 'Hello Dolly,' she said. 'This is a very special cat, I'll have you know. He's a local hero. If it hadn't been for him I'd have been burnt to a crisp in a dreadful fire. He saved my life.'

Feathers was impressed. I could see. Her eyes looked completely round like an owl's. 'Heavens!' she said. 'Did you hear that Bub? This cat's a hero. Imagine that. Was it in the papers?'

'Oh yes,' Leamington Spa said. 'All across the front page.'

'Picture and all,' Jenny said coming back with the chair.

'Heavens!' Feathers said again. 'We couldn't persuade him to star in our show could we?'

'I don't think you can persuade a cat to do anything if my experience is anything to go by,' Toycat Man said. 'They're much too independent. Be good publicity though. He's a handsome animal.'

'If you want him, you can have him,' He said.

That's right! Hand me over like some stupid parcel! Really some people have no idea how to treat a cat. Come on Leamington, leave them. I'm ready for my supper.

But she just stood there, leaning on that old stick of hers and told them the whole story in detail. Which was all very well – I mean we all like a bit of praise now and then – but not when we're starving to death. In the end I had to shout at her to remind her. And they all cheered and clapped their hands. Like I said, they're odd.

It took Potato Boy ages to bring us our food, which was hardly a surprise because the peculiar people were running round the eating room all the time, kissing people and saying 'Wonderful to see you darling! Mwah! Mwah!' and getting in everybody's way. And then just as we were all settling down to our meal and Leamington had cut off a juicy titbit and passed it across the table to me, Feathers came rushing over.

'I've just been talking to Charlie,' she said, 'and it's all arranged. Can I stroke him?'

No, you can't. I'm eating.

'He doesn't like being stroked when he's eating,' Leamington explained.

But she didn't take any notice and stroked me anyway, even though I twitched my fur and gave her a stare to show her not to. Then she looked round the room again.

'Oh look!' she said. 'There's Mrs Turner. Coo-ee Mrs T! I must go and see *her*. I'll tell you all about it presently.' And she went rushing off across the room.

Good riddance.

Leamington Spa cut off a titbit for Kitty and passed it to her, then she found another one for me, which was very tasty so the meal got back to normal. Except of course that the Mwah-Mwahs went on rushing about and shouting. Feathers was the worst. She kept calling things out in a very loud voice so that we all had to listen to her whether we wanted to or not. 'Have you heard our news? Isn't it thrilling? A star my dear! A local hero! The publicity's going to be fabulous.'

One man laughed at her and called out 'You can't direct a cat, Dolly. It's not in the nature of the beast.'

'Don't you believe it, old thing,' she called back, flicking her feathers about. 'Bub could direct anybody. Isn't that right Bub?'

And Toycat Man picked his stuffed cat up by the tail and swung it round his head. How uncouth can people get? I was really quite glad when we'd cleaned Leamington Spa's plate for her and we could jump down and go upstairs - when He wasn't looking - and sit under the radiator. It's nice and quiet in the flat when they're both in the eating room and we needed a nap after our noisy dinner.

It was late and dark by the time Jenny came up to join us. She was so tired she didn't even say hello to us. She just sank down onto the sofa as if the strength had gone out of her and patted the cushions to show us she wanted us to join her. We got up slowly - because it doesn't do to appear too eager, even to someone as nice as her – but then we climbed up one on either side of her and licked her hands and nudged her with our heads to cheer her up. She stroked us both, one with each hand, and said we were the best cats alive, which is true of course but it's nice to hear it said. After that we lay curled up in the warm together and went to sleep again.

Didn't last long. We'd hardly been asleep any time at all before He came crashing up the stairs and started switching on lights and noise machines, which was totally unnecessary, and shouting, 'Am I good or am I good?'

Kitty was frightened out of her life. You could see it. I was quite glad when she picked her up and cuddled her. 'Good at what?' she said in her cool voice.

'I've done a deal,' he said, looking pleased with himself. He goes pink when he's pleased with himself, which is not a pretty sight. That hideous nose of his is bad enough when it's white but it's downright horrible when it's pink.

Jenny looked at him sadly. 'What are you talking about?' she said, stroking my head.

'A deal,' he said. 'That cat takes a starring lead in the panto – they're really keen to have him. You never heard such a fuss. They think he's going to be a draw - and Peacock Pie gets mentioned in all the publicity. You just think what that'll do for trade.'

Oh wonderful, I thought, giving him one of my scathing looks. That's all I need. To be good for trade. That's what cats are for.

'Excuse me,' she said. 'I don't remember you consulting me.'

'Wasn't time,' He said airily. 'You were in the kitchen or somewhere. I had to think quickly. That's the essence of good business, the ability to think quickly. On your feet. That sort of thing. Anyway I knew you wouldn't mind. You're always telling me how wonderful he is.'

'I do mind,' she said. 'Very much. He's not your property to loan out to a gang of strangers whenever you feel like it.'

'He'll be all right,' he said, putting on his pleading face. 'He's only got to walk onto the stage now and then. And they're not a gang of strangers. I mean to say, they're the Bluebells. Oh come on Jen! It's the chance of a lifetime. He's only a cat.'

I could feel her spine stiffening. 'He's not *only a cat*,' she said, 'he's a friend. Best friend I ever had. A lovely, true, dependable friend, aren't you Cat. He kept me company during one of the worst times in my life.'

That's right. You tell him.

'Well anyway,' he said, pressing buttons on yet another machine. 'It's all fixed. God, Do I need a drink or do I need a drink?'

She put Kitty back among the cushions, stood up and walked over to where he stood, still pushing buttons. She didn't say anything. She just took the little machine out of his hand and pressed it once. It was amazing. The machine in the corner stopped shouting and the room went back to being peaceful again. He looked gobsmacked.

'What did you do that for?' he said.

'Now you listen to me,' she said. 'And you listen good. My cat is not a commodity to be bought or sold or loaned or whatever. He's a living sentient creature.'

'It wouldn't hurt him,' he whined. 'He'd probably enjoy it.'

'It might upset him. You don't know. And I'm not having that.'

'But think what an opportunity it is.'

She was on her way back to the sofa and didn't look at him. 'We're going to bed,' she said, picking Kitty up.

'I'm not having two cats in my bed,' he said, looking petty.

'You're not having me in your bed either,' she said, and walked out of the room, carrying Kitty and leaving him with his mouth open. Quite right too. Naturally I followed her. I mean, you can't expect me to stay in a room with him and his noise machines. That's more than any sensitive cat could stand and I'm an extremely sensitive cat. We walked across the hall into a room I'd never seen before. There was a bed up against one wall, heaped with cushions and looking comfortable. She put Kitty down among the cushions and stroked her. 'There you are Kitty,' she said 'Make a little nest.'

Kitty blinked her eyes and looked puzzled. I don't think she knows how to make a nest yet. You can't blame her. She's very young. So I jumped up alongside her and made a nice comfy one for both of us, turning round and round to scoop out a good shape.

*

Well we had a really good night in our new bed and now we're up and in the kitchen and Jenny's put two bowls of that peculiar cat food down for us and we're eating it to show willing, while she stands by the table and sips tea. But better than that, there's no sign of Him. Maybe he's taken the hint and gone somewhere else. Now she's rushing about, chuntering to herself, jamming two great piles of books into that great bag of hers, pushing her hair under a knitted hat and winding a knitted scarf round her neck.

'Be good cats,' she says and then she bends down to stroke us and before we can even purr, she's gone.

I jump up on the window sill to see what sort of day it is and there's a car parked right outside and someone sitting in it gazing at our front door. And while I'm watching, she runs out of the door and the car door opens and Sandyman gets out. He takes her untidy bag and puts it on the back seat and then she gets into the seat in the front and they rub their faces together and the car moves off. How odd. Still at least he's not standing about in the eating room getting in everybody's way.

Kitty's cleaning her whiskers. That cat food is very sticky. When she's finished I shall take her out in the alley and see what we can catch for a real breakfast.

We've had the most peculiar week. He's come over

all kind and friendly all of a sudden. I can't understand it. Every so often He puts on a silly voice and calls out, 'Here, Kitty-Kitty. Here Cat. Come and see what I've got for you. You're gonna love this.' And then he stands there and rattles a paper bag at us and grins at us as if his face has been glued. It's bizarre. We've been ignoring him. Naturally.

When Jen came in this morning and saw what he was doing, she said 'You're never going to win him over that way.'

He changed his glued look at once and scowled at her. 'I'll win him over,' he said. 'You just see if I won't. I'll take him there by the scruff of his neck if I have to.'

She gave him her withering look. 'Well just see you treat him properly while I'm at school,' she said, 'that's all. And don't think I shan't find out if you haven't. I can tell everything I need to know from his little face. Always have done. So I'm warning you.' Then she tickled us behind the ears and picked up that great bag of hers and hauled it through the door.

After she'd gone, he went back to his stupid bag-rattling, so we walked out and left him to it. It was about time for Leroy to arrive, anyway, and the kitchen is a much more salubrious place for a cat than a flat full of moronic noises. There might even be some salmon.

Sandyman walked into the eating room last night

just as we were settling down to roast of the day with Leamington Spa. Wouldn't you know it? It was just as well we'd been served first or we'd have had a long wait. He sort of roamed around as if he was looking for something, so I watched him in between taking titbits from old Leamington and it turned out to be Jenny. The minute she came into the room with four plates balanced on a tray, he shot off through the tables and was beside her before she'd gone more than three steps. He's quick. I'll say that for him.

After she'd delivered the plates, they stood side by side, quite near our table and spoke to one another in very low voices as if they didn't want anyone to hear what they were saying. I can't think why because of course I could hear every word. But then, we cats have exceptionally good hearing. I've told you that before haven't I.

Sandyman said, 'I thought we were going out.'

And Jenny said, 'I *am* sorry but I couldn't let him down. Not when we've got a full house. I mean you can see what it's like, can't you.'

'Hum,' he said. 'So how's the campaign going?'

She screwed up her face as if she'd just bitten on something sour. 'Not good. He keeps saying he'll drag the poor thing there by the scruff of his neck.'

'Hum,' he said again.

'I don't think he will,' she said. 'I mean it's all talk. Throwing his weight about. He wouldn't be so cruel.'

'I you want my opinion,' he said, 'I think he's capable of anything but not to worry. I've got a cunning plan to thwart him.'

She looked up at him. 'It's no joke, Malc.'

'Who says I'm joking? Come out to dinner with me and I'll tell you all about it.'

'I can't.'

'Not even to save your cat from being bullied?'

She looked doubtful. 'Well...'

'Well?'

'I don't know what to do for the best.'

'Take that horrible apron off for a start.'

The potato boy was walking past them with a tray full of dirty plates balanced on the palm of his hand. 'Hang on a minute Kevin,' Sandyman said. 'We've got something else for you to take back to the kitchen. We have, haven't we Jenny?' And she seemed to be thinking hard and then took off her apron and folded it up and put it on top of the plates. Then she and Sandyman walked through the eating room and disappeared.

'Well now, there's a splendid thing Cat,' Leamington Spa said. 'Don't you think so?'

I had no idea what she was talking about. She can be very obscure sometimes. But I gave her my loving look because she had a long strip of beef in her hand and I knew she was going to give it to me. That's the great thing about Leamington Spa. You might not always understand what she's talking about but, if you watch her, you can predict what she's going to do. She's dependable.

I'm beginning to think Sandyman is as weird as all the others. When Kitty and I were strolling out of the eating room last night he suddenly appeared and lifted me up – very gently I must say – and tucked me inside his jacket, which wasn't what I expected at all. Then when I was trying to decide whether to bite him or scratch him so as to get away - because being carried about by Leroy is one thing but that doesn't mean I have to allow everybody to do it – he put his free hand in his pocket and held out a morsel of something very strong-smelling towards me. I took it carefully, after giving it a good sniff, because accepting titbits is not something to be rushed. And it was delicious. He may look odd but he knows how to treat a cat.

Jenny was standing beside us watching it all and when I ate the morsel she put her hand inside the jacket and stroked me and told me I was a good cat. Then they walked out of the front door and into the cold. And it *was* cold. The air was icy. I was quite glad to be inside that coat and up against Sandyman's warm chest. Then the next thing I knew he was easing into his car and sitting down. I have to say he moved very carefully and didn't joggle me about at all. In fact he was almost as good at carrying me as Jenny is. But then she turned a little key and the car juddered and growled and began to move. I wasn't too happy about that to tell you the truth although of course we cats are always valiant in difficult situations so I endured it. And Sandyman stroked me and fed me another tasty morsel that was even better than the first one, so after a while, as I was fairly comfortable and very warm, I settled down inside his coat and waited to see what would happen next.

I didn't have to wait long. We stopped moving after a few minutes and then Sandyman eased out of his seat and carried me into a huge dark room. It was most peculiar, full of seats all arranged in rows and at one end of it there was another room that looked more like a box than a room, with long red curtains hanging on either side of it. That was lit very brightly and there were two Mwah-Mwahs standing in the middle of it talking to one another in the oddest way. Their bodies were far too stiff and their voices sounded as if they didn't mean what they were saying. I told you they were peculiar. Toycat Man was sitting in the middle of one of the rows of seats and when he saw us, he stood up and called out. 'Hold everything! The star's arrived.' Did you ever hear anything so ridiculous? There were only three of them there so they could hardly hold everything and you don't get stars inside a building. I thought everybody knew that.

The light box was instantly full of Mwah-Mwahs all shouting and running about and peering into the darkness. 'Is he coming onstage?' 'Where is he?' 'Oh look, isn't he lovely!'

'Listen up!' Toycat Man said. 'All of you, listen up! We'll run through scene 1 again and see what happens.'

Then they all went mad and started moving the furniture about and a huge canvas sheet came down out of the ceiling and me and Sandyman climbed up some little stairs to see what was happening and Jenny came following after. Sandyman's got a lot of sense. I'll say that for him. He took us well out of the way of all those feet and we stood behind a long black curtain while he stroked me and told me what a good cat I was. Now what?

When they'd stopped moving furniture and somebody had made the lights change colour, one of the Mwah-Mwahs came and stood beside us. He was carrying a long stick over his shoulder with a huge cloth bag dangling from the end of it. I told you they were odd didn't I.

'So what's the score?' he said to Sandyman

Sandyman lifted me out of his jacket and set me down on the floor very gently and Jenny knelt down beside me to give me a stroke and to tell me what a splendid cat I was, which was no more than I deserved. But I kept my eyes open and watched everything, I can tell you, because I don't trust all these Mwah-Mwahs with their big feet.

'Give him one of these before you go on and with luck he'll follow you,' Sandyman said to the stick man. 'Then give him another one when you want to walk off. Same routine. Don't rush him.'

I could hear Toycat Man yelling 'All set?' Why are they all so loud? And a Mwah-Mwah called out, 'Okey-dokey.' And then everything went quiet. And just as I was wondering what would happen next, Stickman knelt right down on the floor beside me and held out the palm of his hand and there was one of those tasty morsels lying right in the middle of it. What an amazing thing! Fancy him having them too.

I didn't take it at once because I'm nothing if not careful but after a little while, when the smell of it was getting to be overpowering, I inched forward and took it – very neatly and carefully, of course. And very tasty it was.

Stickman stood up and arranged his stick on his shoulder. Then he put his hand into his pocket and drew it out with another tasty morsel on it, but then instead of giving it to me, he walked off into the odd room. Well I wasn't having that. I mean to say you can't show a cat a tasty morsel and then walk off and not give it to him. That's not the way to go on. So I followed him.

When he got into the middle of the room he stood still with the morsel still in his hand and started speaking in that silly false way. 'I am too weak to walk another step. My heart I sore and all my strength is gone. This journey is impossible for me. Even with my cat I simply can't go on.'

I gave him a look to show him what nonsense he was talking. I mean he's one of the strongest looking men I've ever seen. Then I sat right in front of him and waited. But all *he* did was sink down on peculiar-looking stone and sigh and say a lot more silly things in that weird voice, which was highly unnecessary. He couldn't have forgotten my morsel. It was still in his hand. I could smell it. I waited for as long as I could because I'm a very patient cat but in the end I reached the limit of my endurance and shouted at him.

And then something extraordinary happened. The Mway-Mwahs went berserk. There's no other word for it. They all suddenly appeared, shouting 'He's a star! A star! Fan-dabby–dowsy!' and running about and hitting one another. They made such a racket it made me jump and I'm not a cowardly cat, not by any manner of means. I was quite relieved when Sandyman strode into the riot and picked me up and put me inside his jacket.

'Shush! Shush!' he said to them in a very commanding voice. 'Remember he's a cat. If you want him to be your star you'll have to treat him gently and not shout.' And at that they actually did shut up but they were still beaming.

By that time, Jenny was standing beside me, stroking my head. 'Time for the off,' Sandyman said to her.

So we went home. And just as well. I'd had quite enough excitement for one day. But like I said, human beings are weird.

CHAPTER 8

I've had the most exhausting week. Never a minute's peace and that's no exaggeration. Not that I ever exaggerate. It would be foreign to my nature. But really! The things that have been happening around here are enough to beggar belief. I can't think what's got into Jenny and the Sandyman.

For a start, we've been to the theatre every single evening. Every single evening. Imagine that. I've hardly settled into my chair for a nap before he comes in and lifts me up and strokes me and says 'Off to the theatre then' and puts me inside his coat. Then Jenny comes in all wrapped up in her chunky jacket and we go downstairs and off we drive. The first time he said it, I didn't know what he was talking about but when we got to this 'theatre' place it turned out to be the peculiar room with all the chairs and the Mwah-Mwahs running about and making a racket and then I knew I was in for some treats so that was all right. I've got them pretty well trained in the treat department now. The Stickman gives me my first one while we're waiting to walk into the light-box and then all I have to do is follow him in and sit and wait while he talks nonsense and then he gives me another one. Sometimes he makes me wait a bit too long and I have to shout at him but I always get what I want. And the Mwah-Mwahs keep quiet. So they've learned how to behave too. They just stand about by the black curtains and watch us. I know because *I* watch *them*. You can never be too careful when it comes to Mwah-Mwahs. But all in all it's a good life.

But then just when I'd got everything sorted to my satisfaction, somebody let a lot of other people into the chair part of the room. I should have known there was something going on when we got to the building because we usually walk in through the empty part of the room past all the chairs and climb up our steps to get to the light-box but yesterday we came through different door and in a different way. It didn't put me off, you understand. I'm too intelligent to be thrown by a change of plan, but it alerted me. We walked past so many rooms and doors I lost count of them, with Mwah-Mwahs rushing in and out, shouting at one another, all in the most peculiar clothes, and somebody calling out 'Overture and beginners please!' I was quite glad to be carried through another door and find we were behind the red curtains, which somebody seemed to have pulled together. It was quiet there. Or quiet for a time. We'd hardly been there two seconds before somebody started to play one of those machines, which was rather unnecessary. It didn't last long, thank heavens. I suppose whoever it was switched it off. But the minute it stopped there was another noise and that *was* alarming. It was a sort of complicated thumping rhythm as if there were lots of people hitting things together. And I could hear voices too.

Jenny was standing right by the red curtain with her eyes right up against the cloth and after a while she turned to Sandyman and said 'It's a good house. I didn't think they'd get so many on the first night.'

'They've come to see your cat,' he said.

'D'you reckon?' she said.

'I know they have,' he said. 'The kids were talking about it in school.'

'Fancy!' she said. But then somebody pulled the red curtains back and Stickman appeared and gave me my first treat and we walked into the light-box. It was very bright out there - much brighter than it's been on the other evenings - so it took a while for my eyes to adjust to the light and on the other side of the red curtain it was completely dark but I could hear people shifting about and talking and a voice saying 'Ah look! There he is!' And then I got my night-sight into focus and saw that the other room was full of people, all sitting in the rows of chairs. How peculiar.

The Stickman had reached his stone and was sitting on it saying his odd words 'I am too weak to walk another step' and all that nonsense, so I sat at his feet and waited for my next treat. I'm nothing if not patient. I was rather surprised when the people in the dark room all started clapping their hands together. Weird! Stickman didn't seem to mind. He looked up and nodded at them and waved his stick and that made them worse. I couldn't have that or he'd forget about the treat, so I shouted at him. And at that they clapped harder and the voice was calling out again. 'Isn't he just cute.' I gave them my stern look to show them they should let him get on with his silly words otherwise he'd forget what he was supposed to be doing and not give me my treat but that made them worse. They went on clapping for such a long time that in the end I had to claw at the Stickman's trousers to remind him. And that made them clap too. I thought I'd never get that treat, the way they were going on. But in the end he woke up to his duties and passed it down to me. And about time too. I ate it in my usual neat way and while I was eating it I heard a loud bell chiming and a very loud voice saying 'Turn again Whittington. Lord Mayor of London.' I stood up and turned my head to see where the noise was coming from and you'll never believe this but I saw Jenny and Sandyman, standing together beside the black curtains on the other side of the light-box. How did they get there? There was nothing to keep me in the light-box now I'd had my treats so I walked off to join them.

'Ah!' the Stickman said. 'I can see I've got to go to London after all. My cat is showing me the way.' And the people clapped and laughed and made a devil of a row and Jenny bent down and stroked me and said I was the cleverest cat alive, which I knew of course but it's nice to have it said.

The Stickman panted up to join us. He was so excited his eyes were popping out of their sockets and the sweat was fairly pouring down his face, which I might say was much too red to be healthy. He looked as though he was melting. There was such a racket going on behind him with people carrying furniture about and a screen creaking down from the ceiling and music playing and somebody singing somewhere, I could barely hear what he was saying. It was all just red-faced babbling. But after a while my ears got used to it and I heard him.

'Did you hear that reception?' he was saying. 'Wasn't it fantastic. What a way to start! Your cat's a natural. Did you see the way he walked offstage? Now that's timing!'

'He's a star,' Jenny said. 'Aren't you Cat?'

Stickman was chortling. 'He's a bloody marvel,' he said. Well of course I am. Everybody knows that and he should have realised it long before now. 'We ought to have him on in the next scene too. D'you think he'd wear it?'

Sandyman made a face. 'Don't push it,' he said. 'He might not like it.'

'I could feed him treats,' Stickman urged. 'Quick. We're on. Say yes. Quick! Quick! Come on!'

'What do you think?' Sandyman said to Jenny.

'Well...' she said, sort of dithering. But before she could say any more the Stickman picked me up and carried me back into the light-box. It was all done so quickly we were there before I could think what he was doing. But he did give me a treat as he carried me in, so he hadn't forgotten his obligations.

The light-box was full of people all walking about and getting in and out of chairs and wearing the most peculiar clothes. There was a man there in stockings and I know that's not right and a girl with a skirt that stuck out on either side of her as if she'd left the clothes hanger in it. Most confusing and to make matters worse they were all talking in that odd stilted way.

The man in the stockings spoke straight to Stickman and called him Dick.

'Ah there you are Dick Whittington,' he said. 'Come in. Now we are gathered here we can begin. Pray to be seated one and all. No ceremony here 'tis freedom hall.' He wasn't making any sort of sense at all but he went on droning away until it made my head spin. Stickman put me down on one of the chairs and gave me another treat and the girl in the peculiar skirt walked over and stroked me, so it wasn't all bad. Except for the silly talking. Eventually, what with the heat from all those lights and being stroked and those dreadful voices droning on and on and on, I dropped off to sleep. I was woken by somebody putting his hand on my back - much too heavily. I opened my eyes at once. It's the cardinal rule of self-preservation to be instantly alert when the need arises. And the need had certainly arisen at that moment because they were talking about me.

'This cat is all the treasure that I have,' Stickman was saying. 'He is a prince of cats and I'd be lost without him.'

Quite right.

But then the Stockingman said something that made my fur stand on end. 'Then *he*'s the very thing that you must send. My rule is firm. I will not break or bend. Each member of my household in indenture must send their treasure to support this venture.'

Send where? What's he talking about?

'He is the prince of mousers,' Stickman said. Quite right. 'King of cats.'

'No more of that,' Stockingman said, putting on a stern face. 'You've got to face the facts. Your cat must join the ship and sail tonight.'

Well I wasn't having that. I don't know what a ship is, truth be told, but I certainly wasn't joining one. The very idea. I jumped down from the chair at once and walked off with my tail in the air. The people in the darkness were clapping their hands and cheering but I hadn't got time to pay attention to them because Jenny and Sandyman were standing by the black curtain and I needed to get to them as quickly as I could. They were rubbing their mouths together – I can't think why they keep doing that. It's so silly – but as soon as they saw me they stopped at once and Jenny picked me up and cuddled me under her chin.

'Oh dear,' she said. 'They've upset him. Look at his poor little face. Oh Malc! I knew this was a bad idea. Look at his poor little face.'

'Home,' Sandyman said. 'We all need feeding. I'll drive this time.'

So we went back to Peacock Pie and she cuddled me all the way and told me I was the best cat ever. And when we got there, Kitty was waiting for me on the stairs the way she always does and Leamington Spa was in the eating room with a plate full of roast beef all steaming hot and ready, so life returned to normal quite quickly.

We've been back in the theatre every night for weeks. Sandyman says I'm a regular old pro. I don't know what a 'pro' is, to tell you the truth, but it's obviously something he approves of because he says it in such a satisfied way and she looks really pleased about it and smiles at him and then he puts an arm round her shoulders and hugs her. The Mwah-Mwahs are as ridiculous as ever, naturally. I never saw such an excitable lot, forever rushing about and shrieking, and as to the way they talk when they're in the light-box, that has to be heard to be believed. Between you and me, I'm beginning to think they're not talking at all, they're just playing games, the way we cats do when we catch a mouse, only not so skilfully of course. They say the same things over and over again and they don't mean a word of them. I'm quite used to being told I've got to 'join the ship and sail tonight' but it never happens.

The chair part of the room in the other hand is full of really sensible people. They've all come to see me, you see, which is gratifying but only to be expected, when you consider how superior I am, and when I walk into the light-box they clap their hands and whistle and cheer and there's always someone who calls out 'Look! There he is! Isn't he wonderful!' But up in the light-box we just do the same silly things over and over again and that gets boring. There are always plenty of treats. I will say that for them. And they've put a chair with a cushion on it next to where Jenny and Sandyman stand so that I can have a nap if I feel like it, which I sometimes do, if it's quiet enough. Trouble is that Jenny and Sandyman will keep talking to one another and it keeps me awake.

He keeps saying 'You ought to leave him, Jenny. You really did.'

And she says 'I can't, Malc. You know that. It would be letting him down.' Which doesn't makes any sort of sense. I mean letting him down what?

After that, they just go on and on. He says she's being taken for a ride, and that's stupid too because they're standing by the black curtain and not riding anywhere. And he says it was the same for him with Wendy.

'We're givers,' he says. 'That's our problem. It puts us at a disadvantage. We're givers and they're takers.'

I wish they'd give me some peace so that I can sleep. Or take me back to the Peacock Pie so that I can have dinner with Leamington Spa.

Tomorrow is the Last Night. Jenny told me when we were driving home. 'Last Night tomorrow', she said, stroking me and giving me her loving look. 'One more performance and then you can retire from the stage and be my lovely cat again. How will that be?'

I gave her *my* loving look because after all I'm always her loving cat even though I don't always know what she's talking about. I think she means it's the last night we shall go to the theatre.

Last Nights are most extraordinary. I could tell things were going to be different the minute we arrived at the theatre and were walking in the back door, because a van drew up and a woman got out with her arms full of flowers, dozens and dozens of them. The smell of them made me sneeze. And that made Sandyman laugh. 'Flowers for the stars,' he said. 'You'll have to get used to that now you're famous.'

There were flowers in every single one of the rooms we passed on our way to the light-box – imagine that - and the Mwah-Mwahs were beside themselves with excitement running about in their peculiar clothes and kissing one another. You'd think they'd never seen flowers before. They should come to the Peacock Pie when He's putting on one of his displays. I was really quite glad to get to the wings where everything was the same as usual. Spoke too soon! Just as I was settling down in my chair one of the Mwah-Mwahs rushed up and kissed me on top of my head and tied a horrible ribbon round my neck. The indignity of it! What does she think I am? A parcel? I scratched it off at once, I can tell you, and gave everybody my cross face. And then Jenny said something that really worried me.

'We're off now Cat. You'll be all right won't you.'

Off? What does she mean off? She's surely not going to leave me here with the Mwah-Mwahs all on my own.

'We're going out front to watch the play,' she said. 'We'll give you a special cheer when we see you.'

I don't want a special cheer, I want her here where I can see her. The Mwah-Mwahs are all very well but you can't trust them.

'See you at the party,' she said and walked away hand in hand with Sandyman, as if I didn't exist. I was flabbergasted. That's the only word for it. Absolutely flabbergasted. I mean she'd always been the one I could trust and now she was walking away from me. Well, I thought, I'm not going to call her back. See if I care. A cat has his pride. She can walk away if she likes. Let her. I shall sit here and wait for my treats.

I got a lot of treats that evening. I think the Mwah-Mwahs were sorry for me. They gave me two treats instead of one, every time, and when I walked into the light-box, the cheers were deafening, so I perked up quite a bit and walked off ahead of the Stickman, the way I always do, and got another rousing cheer. After that everything went as it usually did. I got told I'd 'got to join the ship and sail tonight' and took no notice and the girl with the coat hanger skirt gave me treats and stroked my head and everybody cheered me again. But when I walked out of the light-box there was no one there to pick me up and stroke me and that was miserable. There was nothing for it but to settle down in my chair and have a nap.

I dropped off to sleep pretty quickly, all things considered, but I didn't sleep for very long. I was woken by the sound of something scratching about near my chair and, when I lifted my head, I caught a glimpse of small paws down by the black curtain. There was a mouse sitting within inches of my tail cleaning its whiskers. The effrontery of it. I was off that chair in a spilt second ready to pounce but it was too quick for me, and ran off into the light-box almost before my feet touched the ground. Didn't do it any good though. I'm much too sharp for a mouse to outwit. I ran after it at top speed and had it cornered in no time, even though there were Mwah-Mwahs all over the place getting their silly legs in the way. I gave it a good shaking to stun it and finished it off with a sharp nip to the neck. All very neat and quick. It was very satisfactory. But then all hell broke loose. The people in the dark part of the room were cheering and clapping so loudly you couldn't hear anything else for quite a long time. I kept my paw on the mouse – just in case, you understand. I would have eaten it if it hadn't been for all those people standing around. They were an odd looking bunch and all sorts of colours from sweaty pink through various shades of coffee to quite a nice rich brown. Not as good as Leroy but close. I quite liked the look of him. He was wearing a piece of gold cloth wound round his neck and a long yellow gown and shoes with pom-poms on them and he had his mouth so wide open I could see his tongue.

'Good God!' he said, when the clapping stopped. 'I've never seen anything to equal that.'

The Mwah-Mwah he was talking to gave a huge grin and said. 'I told you he was a good mouser.'

'I know,' Yellow-Gown said. 'But I never thought... I mean ...Wow!'

Then the chair people clapped and laughed so loudly that everybody in the light-box turned to look out at them. And I looked too and there, sitting right in the front, who did I see but Jenny and Sandyman and they were waving at me and calling out. 'Bravo Cat! See you later!' Really the evening was one surprise after another. But then the Mwah-Mwah's started talking in their peculiar way about 'debentures and adventures' and 'the best bargain that you ever made puts all others in the shade' and it went back to being boring again, so I picked up the mouse and walked out of the light-box to find somewhere quiet where I could eat it. And everybody cheered again. They were still cheering when I jumped back into my chair. I've never known them so noisy.

I'd finished my mouse and was cleaning my paws and whiskers when Jenny walked up and stood beside me. I gave her my loving look and waited for her to stroke me but then the red curtains closed and the Mwah-Mwahs came running out of the light-box all talking at once.

'Your cat's a trooper!' Yellow-Gown said. 'To catch a mouse right in front of us and just at the very moment we were talking about him. I've never seen anything to equal it. Never! It was fantastic. What timing! You'll have to bring him on for the final curtain. I mean to say, he's the star of the show. You will won't you.'

But he didn't wait for an answer because they were all rushing off and another lot were walking about in the light-box and the red curtains were opening again. Jenny was laughing at them. 'Clever old thing,' she said to me and she sat down in the chair and patted her knees to show me she wanted me to sit on her lap. Which I did. Naturally.

It was warm and comfortable there so we stayed where we were for a nice long time even though the Mwah-Mwahs were rushing past us all the time and nodding their heads and grinning. I think I had a bit of a nap but I was woken up by such a roar it made me feel dizzy and Stickman and Yellow-Gown were standing in front of us, beckoning, and Jenny was picking me up and carrying me and we all went back into the light-box together. The Mwah-Mwahs were standing in a long line smiling and looking pleased with themselves but they shuffled up and made a space for us right in the middle of the line. And Yellow-Gown took a step forward and held up his hand in the air and the people stopped cheering and clapping and sort of waited.

'Ladies and gentlemen,' he said. 'I give you the star of the show. Dick Whittington's one-and-only, amazing, incomparable, talented, extraordinary Cat.'

Then they went absolutely wild, standing up, stamping their feet, clapping their hands, whistling and cheering, on and on and on. It was only what I deserved, of course, but I have to say it was really rather gratifying. All in all, I think I rather like being in the theatre.

Once everybody had left the light-box and they'd switched off the lights, it was all so empty it looked if nobody had ever been there, so I was quite glad when Jenny said we were going back to Peacock Pie. Sandyman drove the car and I sat on her lap, which was only right and proper. After all, I *was* the star of the show. It didn't take any time at all, which was just as well because I was very hungry by then and needed some sustenance. I wasn't at all sure I'd get any though because it felt like the middle of the night and the eating room would probably be shut but I thought she'd find something for me.

I was wrong. The eating room was full of people all talking to one another, and lots of waiters – more than I'd ever seen. He was poncing about looking smug, although what he'd got to look smug about I couldn't think. But best of all, the tables were absolutely piled with food. I could smell salmon and roast chicken and all sorts of other things. And while I was sniffing the air and trying to work out what they all were so that I could decide which to eat first, who should come walking towards me with a bowl than the cattery-man. And the bowl was full of his special rabbit. He put it down right in front of me.

'Eat up, Cat,' he said. 'You've earned it tonight.'

I didn't need to be told. I ate every mouthful and licked the plate clean. It was delicious and just what I needed. When I'd finished and I was cleaning my paws - I'm always fastidious about hygiene - I took a look round. There were Mwah-Mwahs all over the place, holding plates full of food and glasses full of wine and eating and talking and squealing. It exhausted me just to look at them. And then a man with a complicated black box in his hands appeared in front of me and pointed the box right at me and, while I was trying to remember where I'd seen it before, it flashed all of sudden and so brightly it hurt my eyes. I blinked and gave him my cross look but he didn't take any notice. He just fiddled with the front of the box and made it flash again. And then it was just flash, flash, flash, for absolutely ages. In the end Jenny picked me up very gently and cuddled me under her chin and told him to stop.

'I think that's enough,' she said. 'He's had a long day.'

'One more,' the man said. 'Last one. You make a great shot together.'

'All right then,' she said. 'But just one, mind. That's all.' And the box flashed again.

The Mwah-Mwahs started to sing, the way they'd

been doing when I first saw them, only this time they were jumping about and kicking their legs in the air, which looked downright dangerous. The man with the box went rushing off to flash his horrid light at *them*. And about time too. I took myself off upstairs and left them to it. And luckily the spare room door was open so I went in and jumped up on the bed and settled myself for the night. I'd really had quite enough for one day. There *are* limits, even for a cat with my patience.

CHAPTER 9

After all the excitement at the theatre, it's been rather boring at the Peacock Pie. Jenny goes to that school place of hers, He shouts and rushes about in the kitchen, and me and Kitty just get on with our lives in our usual way. Leroy feeds us whenever He's not about and then we settle down in one of our warm places and have a nap. We go outside to find a suitable digging place whenever we need to but, apart from that, we stay indoors, especially if it's raining. It's been raining a lot, sometimes in a nasty pervasive drizzle but often in a heavy downpour that leaves puddles in the yard and makes the earth sticky, which is very inconvenient when you're digging holes. But apart from that, nothing has happened. Until this morning.

He was so excited when he got out of bed that he didn't even tell me to get off, he just rushed about rubbing his face with his machine and splashing water on himself and throwing clothes about. Jenny stayed where she was among the pillows and watched him while she stroked me and Kitty.

'Right. I'm off,' he said, pulling on one of his smelly jackets. 'Now we shall see.'

'Bring me some chocolate,' she said. But he'd

already gone, banging the door behind him. Uncouth creature. I hope he stays out for hours, wherever he's going.

We stayed where we were in the warm for a nice long time. But in the end she said she'd better get up or she'd be late for school and swung her long legs out of the bed. Me and Kitty were having a stretch ready to follow her when we heard the front door bang and the sound of his great feet thumping up the stairs. By the time he charged into the bedroom he was roaring. He had a paper in his hand and he was shaking it about like a dog killing a rat.

'Look at it!' he shouted. 'Look at the damned thing. We don't get so much as a mention. Not one single miserable mention. I did all this for the publicity and there isn't any.'

Jenny was pulling clothes out of the wardrobe and didn't look at him. 'Did all what?' she said and her voice was cold.

'Did all what?' he shouted. 'What d'you mean, did all what? You know what I did. I let them have that damned cat because they would keep on about it and they promised me faithfully I'd get good publicity. Promised me! And now look. Not so much as a mention. It's all about that damned cat. Look at it! Two pages full of pictures of a stupid cat and Peacock Pie's not mentioned once. Not once. I've a good mind to sue them.'

She put her clothes over her arm neatly. 'I think we'd better get something clear,' she said. '*You* didn't let them have my cat, *I* did and more fool me. I never thought much of it for an idea, as you'll remember. But I agreed to let him go because you made such a thing about it and you were doing my head in. Don't blame me if he turned out to be the star of the show. That was all due to his intelligence. You should have been there on Saturday and you'd have seen that for yourself. He was superb. I'm not a bit surprised they're featuring him in the paper. He's earned it. He's a very clever cat.' And she turned to tickle me under the chin. 'Aren't you my darling?'

Well of course I am.

'Clever cat!' he mocked. 'He's just an ordinary mog. That's all he is. A common or garden ordinary mog. I'm sick to death of the way you slobber over him.'

She narrowed her eyes. 'And I'm sick to death of the way you shriek and roar when you don't get your own way.'

'I've got every right to roar,' he roared. 'I was promised publicity and they've reneged on their promise. We're not talking about the cat. He's just a nuisance. We're talking about the way I've been treated.'

'OK. They took you for a ride,' she said. 'It happens. Get over it.'

His face was dark red and covered in sweat. 'Get over it!' he roared. 'Get over it! I'll sue them. That's what I'll do. Sue them. Damn people. They needn't think they can treat me like this and get away with it.'

And he threw the paper on the floor and kicked the bed.

He hurt his foot. Serve him right. What did he expect? Great clumsy oaf! Me and Kitty watched him from the pillows as he jumped about all over the room shrieking and swearing and holding his ankle. But Jenny laughed at him. It was a mistake. It made him so furious he didn't know what to do with himself and he took his anger out on us.

'Got those damned cats off the bed,' he shouted and he picked Kitty up by the scruff of the neck and threw her across the room. Poor little thing. She landed neatly but she was so surprised she had eyes like an owl. I got off the bed at once, in one movement. Not because I was afraid of him - I'm not the sort of animal to be afraid of anything, you understand, and he's just a howling oaf – no, no, I moved because I didn't want to be hurled about too. He was in such a foul temper he was quite capable of it. I walked across to poor Kitty and gave her a lick to encourage her and we left the room together with our tails in the air.

As we lolloped down the stairs I could hear Jenny shouting at him. 'You really are the most heartless, unfeeling, selfish, greedy nerd. How dare you throw that poor little cat about!'

He was shrieking. 'God damn it! You're in *my* house. I won't be spoken to like that in *my* house.'

We dodged into the kitchen as fast as we could and hid in the cupboard among the saucepans. And not a minute too soon because He came roaring in as soon as we'd found a more or less comfortable space.

He was shouting, 'You're late!' so somebody else must have come in with him.

It was Potato-boy. 'No I ain't,' he said. 'Eight o'clock, you said, an' it's eight o'clock exact. Look at the clock if you don't believe me.'

'And that's enough of your lip,' He shouted. 'If I say you're to be here on time, you're to be here on time and there's an end of it. We shall have the delivery van here any minute.'

'They're here now.' Potato-Boy said and they both went stomping off.

It was time to find a better hiding place. I edged out of the cupboard just in case there was anyone else there and me and Kitty slipped out into the yard like a pair of shadows and jumped over the fence into the alley. The dog in the fourth yard along went berserk and threw himself at the fence but we didn't take any notice of him. Dogs are always barking themselves silly. It's the way they go on. We just trotted past him and kept on going until we reached the green, where we caught ourselves a bit of breakfast, one scraggy starling, which was all bones and an elderly mouse that was a bit too tough for my taste. Better than nothing though. We wouldn't have got anything at all if we'd stayed in the Peacock Pie.

We spent the rest of the day on the green where it was safer. There was a pile of old cardboard boxes under the hedge and we made a nest of them.

Nowhere near warm enough but it kept the rain off. We didn't go back to Peacock Pie until it started to get dark. By then we were both jolly hungry, I can tell you, but I reckoned He ought to have got over all that roaring by then and with a bit of luck Leroy would be there.

He was. What good timing. But then I've always had a superb sense of timing. Not that I brag. Most cats have good timing and mine is superlative. They said so at the theatre and they were quite right.

But I was reckoning without Him. Leroy was really pleased to see us and fed us some tasty slithers of salmon and a plate full of chicken skin but just as we were settling in to enjoy our supper there was a horrible roar and there He was, red in the face, shouting and pointing. 'Get those damned cats out of here. I don't pay good money to feed *them*.'

'They no problem,' Leroy said. 'They eat de scrap. We don' mind. It onny go to waste.'

'I mind,' he shouted. 'Get them out of here.'

'I put in de yard for you,' Leroy said to us, picking up the plate.

'You're not listening to me,' He said. 'When I say you're not to feed them, you're not to feed them. Just kick them out in the yard and get back to what you should be doing. I don't pay you good money to pander to a couple of lousy mogs.'

'You wan' watch what you sayin' man,' Leroy said. 'You don' pay me good. You pay me *pittance*.'

'I pay you the going rate,' He said, 'and don't you

forget it. So let's have a little less of your mouth.'

'Mout'!' Leroy said. He was really angry. You could tell by the way he straightened his back and the way his hair was bristling. 'Mout'! Now *you* lissen, man. I don' take no crap from no one. No one. You unnerstan'.'

'I'm the boss,' He said. His face was dark red again and sweaty. 'I can say what I like.'

'Right!' Leroy said. 'I ain' stoppin' here to be abuse. I quit.'

He closed his face, shrugged his shoulders and walked away. 'Suit yourself,' he said.

Leroy walked to the row of lockers without another word, opened one of them and pulled out a long bag while everybody in the kitchen stopped and watched him. He took off his apron and his chef's hat, folded them and put them in the bag. Then he stroked me and Kitty and tickled us under the chin, put the bag over his shoulder and walked out of the door. Potato-Boy's eyes looked as if they were going to pop out of his head but he didn't say anything and nor did anyone else.

I reckoned it was time to get out before they all started shouting and banging again, so we snatched what we could from the plate and ran into the eating room before anyone could stop us. And there was dear old Leamington Spa, sitting in her usual corner with her napkin over her knees and our chairs waiting for us on the other side of her table. I was really glad to see her.

'Hello, you two pretty creatures,' she said. 'It's pork tonight.'

It was delicious and He didn't put in an appearance for once, so we enjoyed it a lot. Leamington Spa didn't eat very much of it so we cleaned her plate for her, which was very good of us. She said so. But, when Potato-boy came to the table to ask her what she wanted for her sweet, she said she wasn't feeling quite the thing.

'I think I'll give it the go-by tonight,' she said.

And he said 'Okey-dokey' and walked away from us.

But then a very odd thing happened. Leamington Spa reached for her stick and stood up, sort of wobbling. We watched her as she started to walk between the tables and she was wobbling all over the place, as if she didn't know where she was going. We got down from our chairs as soon as she'd gone, of course, and walked off toward the stairs. There was no point in us staying in the eating room if there wasn't going to be any more food. But we'd hardly covered any ground at all before there was a crash and when I looked back, Leamington Spa was lying on the carpet with her eyes shut. She'd got the edge of one of the table-cloths in her hand and she'd pulled the cloth and everything on it down on the floor beside her. People were standing up to get a better view and the waiters were all rushing towards her looking startled and there was such a noise and such a lot of movement I thought we'd better get out of it as soon as we could. Which we did.

But when we got upstairs, we ran into difficulties.

For a start, Jenny wasn't in the flat. We looked everywhere and there wasn't a sign of her. Not so much as a sniff. Not even a coat flung across the bed or shoes kicked off on the rug or a towel dropped on the floor and there's usually something like that when she's back. It was most peculiar because she's always there at night time. Always. I've never known her not be there at night time. To make matters worse, there was nowhere to hide until she *did* come back. The door to the spare room was shut. I couldn't scratch it open no matter how hard I tried and I knew that if we settled on any of the chairs or the sofa or the bed, He'd be sure to throw us off, given the mood he was in, and I didn't want poor Kitty to be flung about for a second time. In the end I decided it would be better for us to go out in the yard and wait for her there. We could watch her window and see her when she pulled the curtains. So that's where we went.

We waited for hours and hours in the dark watching that window. Never took our eyes off it for a second. But she didn't come home and gradually all the houses around us put out their lights and it was deep night and everything was quiet except for the sound of an occasional car in the road beyond the buildings. So I had to accept that she hadn't come back, miserable though that was, and that nothing could be done about it until the morning.

It was murderously cold by then and raining in a

horrid drizzle that stuck to our coats and was hard to shake off, so we obviously had to find some sort of shelter, otherwise we'd have been frozen solid by morning. There was nothing in the yard except dustbins and they weren't any use to us at all, so we went back to the green to see if our cardboard nest was still there and it was, so we eased into the middle of it, huddled up together to keep warm and settle to sleep there. It wasn't the easiest night I've ever spent, to tell you the truth, although Kitty didn't seem to mind it. I was quite glad when the sun came up and the birds started to sing.

We were both a bit stiff when we eased out of our nest but we had a quick wash and set off to Peacock Pie again. She must be home by now. And she'd let us in and feed us and cuddle us and it would all be back as it was. But when we got to the yard there was still no sign of her and it took a very long time before someone opened the kitchen doors so that we could get in. It was very cold waiting about, especially as were hungry, but in the end a new boy came out with a pile of cardboard in his arms so we slipped in while he was struggling to open the nearest bin. Didn't do us any good because there was a new cook there too, a horrible beefy looking man with red pimples all over his face, and he started to roar the minute he saw us.

'Out! Out! I don't have cats in my kitchen.'

Potato-boy tried to speak up for us. 'They're no trouble,' he said. 'They eat the scraps. Leroy used to…'

But Pimples wouldn't let him finish. Horrid man.

'Leroy's gone,' he shouted. 'Right! Understand that! Leroy's gone and *I'm* here now. Just get rid of them. Damned things. They're unhygienic.'

He's a fine one to talk about hygiene with a face covered in pustules. I mean, yuk! He should try looking in a mirror if he wants to see something really unhygienic. And someone should tell him that cats are the cleanest animals on the planet. Not that anybody had the gump to tell him anything. They were all too busy keeping out of his way. So we had to get out and keep out of his way too. We slid into the hall, very quietly, when they weren't looking, and crept up the stairs, keeping our bellies low, just in case. It was all useless. Jenny wasn't in the flat and everything was exactly the same as it had been the night before. I couldn't understand it. I mean, she's *always* there. She wouldn't leave us. Not Jenny. Anyone else but not her. But there wasn't time to think about it, even for a second, because we could hear Him stomping up the stairs towards us, so we hid under the bed until he'd gone crashing out again. Trouble was, we didn't feel safe, even then. Not on our own. So we went back to the yard and kept out of harm's way.

The rain went on all morning and there was no food. It was really no way to treat a cat of my calibre. Stuck out there in the rain with a nasty cold wind blowing my fur up the wrong way and no food. But we waited in the yard for ages and watched the window just in case she came back because we're nothing if not patient. She never did though. But towards evening, when it was beginning to get dark and we could hear people arriving in the eating room, I was visited with thoughts of brilliance.

We could go and see Leamington Spa. Of course. That's what we'd do. Go and see dear old Leamington Spa. She always came back to her room around this sort of time and she'd be good for a saucer of milk to keep us going, and the heat machine to warm us up, if nothing else, and then we could all go back to Peacock Pie together and they'd be bound to let us in if we were with her. It was a master plan. So off we went.

Kitty was beginning to flag, poor little thing. Hunger pains I expect. Young cats can't withstand hunger the way we mature ones can. But she kept up gamely and it didn't take us long to reach the house. We were in luck. The front door was ajar. We didn't have to sit under the privet hedge and wait. We could walk straight in.

There were a lot of people in the hall, all standing about as if they were waiting for something and all smelling very peculiar. There were so many strong, strange smells in that small space it made my head dizzy. But they were very friendly and some of the girls bent down to stroke us so we went and sat outside Leamington Spa's door and looked hopeful.

'Never knew you had cats,' one of the boys said. 'I thought pets were banned.'

'They are,' one of the girls said. 'That black one sort of belongs to the old lady. I've seen it round here lots a' times. It comes to visit her.'

'I thought she'd gone to hospital,' another boy said.

'She has,' the girl said and she knelt down and stroked my back, which was very pleasant. 'You're out of luck tonight cat.'

I miaowed at her prettily and looked at the door again. Maybe she'd open it for us if we asked her nicely. She seemed the sort of girl who could take a hint.

She was still kneeling on the floor and still stroking me but she looked over her shoulder at a stout man in a smelly jersey. 'It wants to go in,' she said. 'You got a key Tony?'

'I'm not supposed to,' he said. 'You know the rules.'

'Pretty please?' the girl said. 'We can't leave it out in the hall crying.'

I miaowed again, to prove her point. Then I waited because I'm very patient. It's one of my great strengths.

He considered for an unnecessarily long time, then he said, 'Oh all right then. As it's you,' produced a fistful of keys and opened the door.

The room was empty. You could smell that Leamington Spa had been there but there was no sign of her. And the fire machine was off. We'd come all this way and we were starving hungry and she wasn't there. No Jenny, no Leroy, no Leamington Spa, no food. There was nothing for it. If there was no one to give us food, I would have to go hunting.

It was a bad time for hunting. Too dark to see well for a start, even though my eyesight is superlative and too wet and too cold to let us pick up a scent. We went back to the alley because there are often mice there, scuttling about among the bins but I only saw three and they were too quick for me. The last one slipped through a gap in the fence and disappeared into one of the back yards. I stood on the wrong side of the fence and listened and I could hear rustling and scrabbling. Now that was better. If I could just find a gap big enough for me to get through I might be in with a chance of a kill.

It took a little while but in the end I found the gap I wanted and squeezed through. I was in luck. Someone had knocked a bin over. It was lying on its side spilling all sorts of foul-smelling things onto the concrete and there were mice everywhere. I could take my pick of them and did, neat, quick and deadly, before half of them knew I was there.

Then everything went hideously wrong. There was a frenzy of barking and an absolutely huge dog was charging into the yard, showing its teeth and slavering.

Out! Be quick! No time to find the gap. Can't even see it. Quick! Quick! Up and over the fence with the mouse between my teeth and the dog snapping at my tail. Something sharp tore at my belly as I reached the top but I couldn't stop. One more effort and I'd slithered down the safe side of the fence and was back in the alley again. I'd escaped.

I was so out of breath I dropped the mouse but luckily Kitty picked it up and finished it off. I let her eat it because she was very hungry and I was out of breath and had such a pain in my belly I couldn't fancy eating. Couldn't even think straight. All I wanted to do was lie down. And I couldn't lie down in the alley because it was raining again.

Dragged back to the nest. Took a long time. A very long time. I think Kitty went on ahead of me but I wasn't sure. Too tired to be sure. Could barely move my legs. And my belly hurt. I wanted to lie down. And sleep and sleep.

CHAPTER 10

I don't know how long I've been asleep, but I do know it's been a long time. I woke a few minutes ago and I was feeling so stiff and cold I couldn't stand. It was freezing even under our cardboard boxes and I could hear the rain falling, tap, tap, tap, on top of us. There was somebody calling too, 'Kitty, kitty, kitty' and 'Cat where are you?' but it sounded a long way away and I hadn't got the energy to get up and see who it was. Kitty was on her feet, miaowing and peering out into the rain, but all I wanted to do was sleep.

After a while I could hear feet approaching and a hand reached into our nest and stroked Kitty and picked her up. I could smell Jenny's skin and hear her voice, so I knew she must have come back but even then I couldn't get up on my feet. Or call to her.

'Hold on to Kitty for me,' her voice said. 'He must be in here somewhere. If I just lift...' And I made a great effort and opened my eyes and there she was, looking down at me. It made me feel weak to see her but I managed a purr. She lifted me up very gently with both hands and tucked me under her chin.

'He's soaking wet, Malc.'

Now I could hear Sandyman. 'They both are,' he said. 'This one looks as if she's been thrown in the bath. Have you still got the basket? We ought to get them home...'

I was drifting off to sleep again. I couldn't help it. I didn't even have the strength to go on purring. But I could hear Jenny's voice and she sounded upset. 'He's hurt Malc. He's bleeding. Look...' Then I was sort of washed away.

When I woke up again we were all in the car. I was lying on her lap, wrapped up in something warm and she was stroking my head and Kitty was in the cat basket beside us washing herself. I have to say it felt good, even though I *was* tired. I'd had quite enough of being out in the rain.

The next time I woke, Jenny was carrying me into a white room that smelt very peculiar. I'd have been alarmed if I hadn't been so tired. As it was, I lay on the table where Jenny'd put me, half awake and half asleep, while she talked to a girl in a long white coat. Odd words like 'bleeding' 'nasty cut' 'broken glass' 'stitches' 'antibiotics' filtered down to me out of a swimming medley of noises, but they didn't mean anything. Something stung my neck and the girl in the white coat was turning me on my side and peering down at my belly but then I was asleep again and drifting. I think I drifted for a very long time because when I woke up I was in a cage and I could feel something uncomfortable round my neck and see something white sticking out on either side of my face, blocking my view. It was all very peculiar. It didn't worry me you understand. We cats are the calmest of creatures. But it *was* peculiar. And very uncomfortable.

Presently I became aware of a face peering at me through the bars. Not a bad face. In fact rather a kindly one. 'And how are you this morning Cat?' it said. 'Let's have you out of there and see, shall we?'

It was another girl in a white coat. She lifted me out of the cage very gently and put me down on a table and stroked my head. Then a man in a white coat came in and told me I was a good cat, which was only true and to be expected, and bent down and looked at my belly, smoothing the fur and looking serious.

'Yes,' he said.' That's healing nicely.'

Then he did an absolutely appalling thing. You'll find it hard to believe, I know, but it's true. He held me down with one hand and pushed something hard and unpleasant right up my backside with the other. The indignity of it! Naturally, I put up a tremendous fight. I swore and snarled and tried to kick him and bite him, but it took him a long time to understand that he was to stop it. I won in the end, naturally, because I went on swearing and biting until he did what I wanted and took the horrid thing out. But really, the insensitivity of it. To do such a vile thing to a cat of my calibre. It beggars belief. The girl in the white coat stroked me and told me I was a good cat but I was very, very annoyed and kept my hackles up until he'd gone away.

That took a while too. He stood with the horrible

thing in his hand, squinting at it for far too long. But at last he said. 'Yes, that's fine. He's ready to sign off. I'll prescribe some more antibiotics and he can go.'

I was absolutely exhausted. So the white-coat girl put me back in my cage on my warm blanket to let me have a sleep. And quite right too, after all I'd been through.

The next time I woke up, Jenny was smiling down at me and the door of the cage was open.

'Hello Cat,' she said, putting her hand into the cage to stroke me. 'Are you ready to come home?' And when I licked her hand to show her how glad I was to see her, she lifted me out of the cage, very gently and put me in the cat-basket. I didn't make a fuss about it. It wasn't the time and anyway it smelt good after all the strange smells in the cage.

The next time I woke up, the cat-basket was standing on a carpet right in front of a lovely warm fire and Kitty was sitting beside it waiting for me. I eased out of the basket in my delicate way and sat in front of the fire. It was blissful. And while I was sitting there and Kitty was washing my tail for me, like the friend she is, Sandyman appeared with a bowl full of water and another with some very tasty-smelling food in it and laid them down right in front of me. Wasn't that kind. I've got a lot of time for Sandyman.

It took a while to eat the food because I could only manage a few mouthfuls at a time, but the water was very welcome. Afterwards me and Kitty curled up in front of the fire and had a nice long sleep together. If this is home, I'm all for it.

Me and Kitty have explored this place from top to bottom and it's not a flat but a house and a very good one, almost purpose built for cats, and you can't say that about most places. There are lots of sunny spots, comfortable chairs, a very big bed where we can sleep during the day while they're out at their school place and, outside the kitchen door, a garden where there are lots of trees and all manner of corners to hide in and all sorts of things growing and *no dogs*. If it weren't so cold, we'd be out there all the time because there's a little door called a cat flap, at just the right height in the proper door and it's especially for us. Sandyman said so. All we have to do is nudge it open with our heads and we can walk straight outside and dig and hunt whenever we want to. Not that we need to hunt, because the food here is splendid and plentiful. Jenny and Sandyman spend every evening in the kitchen cooking things for us and me and Kitty sit on the work surfaces and help them by looking encouraging and then we all go off into the dining room and share it between us. At first, it was quite difficult to eat with that silly collar getting in the way but they've taken it off now, so I eat as much as I like.

'This is the life, Cat,' Sandyman says, when we all settle down on the sofa in front of the fire of an evening. He and Jenny watch a noise machine that flickers and shouts, which is a bit of a drawback sometimes, but they seem to enjoy it so we don't complain.

Then he says, 'Glad you moved?' to Jenny.

And she says 'Best thing I ever did', and gives him a kiss.

'Wait till Easter comes,' he says. 'We'll have some fun then. We'll put the hammock up.'

'Kitty'll be fully grown by that time,' she says, 'and we shall have two big handsome cats.'

It's so good to be appreciated. I wonder who Easter is.

It's not a 'who', it's a time. And you know it's come because the garden is full of yellow flowers. Sandyman came into the kitchen yesterday with a great bunch of them. They're called daffodils. I seem to remember them from last year but I'm not entirely sure. Jenny put them in vases full of water and carried them all into the dining room and stood them on the table. It was quite a job to for me and Kitty to find a space for our morning nap. We managed it eventually of course. We're nothing if not resourceful.

But we'd barely had forty winks before Jenny came and started calling for Sandyman. 'Malc! Malc! Do come and see this.'

He came in with a trowel in his hand and stood in the doorway looking at us.

'Aren't they splendid,' she said. 'Two cats among the daffodils. And if that's not a sign of spring I'd like to know what is.'

He took one of those little boxes out of his pocket, the ones they're always tapping and looking at, but he didn't tap this one or look at it much, he pointed it at us. Me and Kitty stayed where we were because we were very sleepy and we don't mind little boxes because they don't flash lights at you, they just make a little click. Which it did.

'There you are,' he said. 'Now you've got the moment on record.'

'I do love you,' Jenny said.

'More than the cats?' he asked, smiling at her.

'Well I wouldn't go as far as to say that,' she said, smiling back. 'But close.'

'Then if that's the case,' he said, 'I think we ought to tie the knot.'

What knot? What's he talking about?

'Well maybe,' Jenny said. 'I shall have to discuss it with the cats.'

'You could have daffodils in your bouquet,' Sandyman said. And that set them off into one of their meaningless duets. Human beings are very prone to meaningless duets.

'I'd rather have roses.'

'Good. 'You're on!'

'Is that a proposal?'

'If you'd like it to be.'

'I don't see you down on your knees.'

'If I were down on my knees, I couldn't kiss you.'

'You've got a point.'

Like I said, 'meaningless'. If that was the way they

were going on, it was a waste of time listening to them. And they'd reached the stage when they start rubbing their faces together, and that's so boring it's not worth watching them either. Me and Kitty went back to sleep and left them to get on with it.

It's wonderfully warm. Has been for days and days. Me and Kitty spend most of our time in the garden snoozing in the sun. Actually, it's the best place to be because the house is full of demented people all running about squealing and putting absolutely ridiculous hats on their heads, all long feathers on stalks and soppy looking flowers and bits of gauze like spiders' webs, as if they've been hunting in the long grass. There were so many of them in the kitchen yesterday afternoon, me and Kitty couldn't get in through the cat flap because of all their feet. And this morning it got worse. Although I have to admit, the day started well enough.

Sandyman got up as soon as I'd given him a nudge to remind him and shuffled round the room scratching his head and struggling into his dressing gown the way he usually does and then the three of us went downstairs to breakfast and left Jenny to finish her sleep.

It was peaceful in the kitchen with the sun shining through the windows to warm our coats and lots of food in our dishes. When we'd eaten every last crumb, we jumped up on the table and watched Sandyman while he drank his coffee and stroked us.

After a while there was a quiet tap on the door and who should it be but the Catteryman. To tell you the truth – and I always tell the truth, we cats are the most truthful animals ever born - I didn't recognise him at first because he was wearing a grey suit and a tie. Imagine that! But as soon as he put out his hand to stroke me, I knew exactly who he was because he smelt the same even in his weird clothes. A dependable creature, the Catteryman, and he doesn't wear silly things on his head. We all sat round the kitchen table like old friends and there were two of them to stroke us and admire us, which was exactly as it should be. Too good to last though. We'd hardly had any time together at all before someone rang the doorbell, on and on and on, as if their fingers were stuck to the silly thing, and we could hear lots of voices, all very excitable, squeaking and squealing. It made me shiver my fur with horror just to hear them and, when they came crushing into the kitchen, things got just too horrible for words.

They filled every single space in it, what with their stupid great hats filling the air and their stupid great feet trampling all over the floor and their stupid arms waving and grabbing one another, and the way they kept rushing about. And they were so loud. If there'd been half an inch of clear space on the floor where I wouldn't have got kicked or trampled on, I'd have been off the table and out of the house before you could blink. But there wasn't, so I had to stay where I was and me and Kitty had to try to keep out of harm's way behind the coffee-pot, which wasn't the best of places, I can tell you. Some of them were from the theatre, of course, and theatre people are wickedly unpredictable. I saw Feathers straight away, rushing at Sandyman. She had a flowerpot and two enormous wings on her head. It must have been a very big bird. I wonder what she did with the rest of it. Ate it probably.

'Malcolm! Malcolm! My dear boy!' she shrieked. 'What are you *doing* still in your jim-jams?'

Sandyman grinned at her. 'Drinking a cup of coffee,' he said.

'Coffee!' she shrieked. 'You can't sit about drinking coffee. Look at the time. You ought to be dressed.'

'There's plenty of time,' he said. 'Hours yet.' But she pulled him out of his chair and frog-marched him to the door, while all the others cheered as if she'd done something wonderful. Now perhaps they'd all follow him out and me and Kitty can get a bit of peace and quiet. But no! That horrible doorbell was ringing again. Oh for heaven's sake! Not more people.

It was a girl in a green apron carrying a box full of white carnations and a big bunch of red and white roses, tied up with a white ribbon. They cheered her into the kitchen and made a space for the box next to the coffee-pot. So that was our hiding place gone and there was nothing we could do except jump down and sit on Sandyman's empty chair and hope none of them would notice us. It was a faint hope.

Toycat Man had sprung into action in his awkward way – his arms and legs are like broom handles - handing out carnations to them all and making a great fuss of it. Why can't human beings do things quietly? There was no need for all that shouting and shrieking. But no. They couldn't even put a carnation into a buttonhole without squealing and Toycat Man was poking about inside the box and yelling 'Where's the ribbons? I can't find the ribbons?' until I thought my ears would split. Two of the others rushed over to help him and turned the box upside-down and shook it, scattering leaves and petals all over the table until they finally found two long white and gold ribbons in the wreckage and held them up to cheers and whistles. I know I've said it before, but really, human beings are the most peculiar creatures. But what happened next was so appalling you'll never believe it. They came chirruping over to Sandyman's chair, grabbed hold of me and Kitty and tied those dreadful ribbons round our necks. The indignity of it. The thoughtlessness. The stupidity. I swore and snarled at them, and kicked at them and tried to scratch them, and did everything I could to make them stop but they just went on and on until the horrible things were tied. I was so cross I could barely breathe. And then several things happened all at once.

Sandyman came back in a grey suit with a red tie round his neck and got pounced on by Feathers and had a red carnation pinned to his lapel, and then the doorbell rang again and three more people came in, a young man in a grey uniform and a cap with a black brim, who walked across to Sandyman and said, 'Cars are here, sir.' And behind him, Leroy and the Potato Boy - what do you think of that? - grinning fit to crack their faces.

'We com' wid de feast,' Leroy said to Sandyman in his comfortable drawling way. 'Where you wan' me put it'?' Then he saw me and walked across to stroke me.

'Hi dere, Cat,' he said, stroking me. 'You lookin' good. How you doin'?

I scowled at him. I am *not* looking good. How could I possibly look good wearing this ridiculous ribbon? I thought he had better sense. But he was looking at Sandyman again. And Sandyman was saying 'Yes, yes. The breakfast. Yes of course.' And looking at the man in the funny hat, who was saying, 'Ready for the off, sir?' and saying, 'Yes, yes, of course' in the same undecided way. What was the matter with him? He'd always been such an easy sort of man. I've never seen him fuss about anything. And now there he was, standing in the middle of the kitchen as if he was glued to the spot, twittering.

'Come on, Malc,' Catteryman said to him, grinning and taking his arm. 'Time you were going or you'll be late. Dolly'll look after the meal, won't you Dolly?'

'Course!' Feathers said, nodding her head so that her wings flapped. 'Leave it to me.' And she gave

Sandyman a little push towards the door. 'Good luck! We'll all be following you.'

He went but he was still looking puzzled although Catteryman was thumping him on the back and saying 'Come on Malc!' in the most encouraging way. And as soon as they'd gone, Feathers led Leroy and the Potato Boy out of the room, calling back at the others. 'Look sharp, you lot. Ten minutes!' which didn't do any good at all because it just sent them into a paroxysm of shrieks and yells. They were so loud they made my ears ache, even though I'd put them back as far as they would go. And they frightened Kitty so much she hid under the table.

They went on for hours, rushing about, and waving their arms, and shouting at one another and then all of a sudden Toycat Man yelled. 'Onwards and upwards!' and they made a dash for the door and charged through. The kitchen was so quiet I could hear the clock ticking and a robin singing in the garden. I was totally exhausted.

Kitty crawled out from under the table and began to wash her face like the sensible cat she is and, as she was setting me such a good example, I followed it. We were still washing our whiskers when the door opened and Jenny came in, looking very pretty in a white suit and a dear little white hat. *She* doesn't wear dead birds on her head, I'm glad to say. She had a friend with her I'd never seen before and she was all dressed in blue, even down to her shoes and carrying a tray full of breakfast things, which she put down on the table. 'There's the car,' she said. 'All set?'

Jenny smiled at her. 'I've just got to say goodbye to the cats,' she said, and bent down to stroke us both, one after the other. Me first of course, which was only right and proper because I *am* the senior cat. 'Be good little cats,' she said, 'and when I come back I'll give you some treats. I promise.'

Then she picked up the big bunch of flowers and held it in front of her like a sort of shield and she and her friend walked arm in arm out of the kitchen into the hall and were gone. Now we could get rid of those stupid ribbons, which we'd have done earlier if we'd had a chance, because no self-respecting cat ever wears a ribbon. Ever. After all, we're not dogs. It took some doing because they'd tied them much too lightly, but with a bit of biting and tearing we managed it in the end. Then we went off on a tour of inspection to make sure they'd all gone.

And you'll never believe this but we found the treats. She hadn't hidden them in the cupboard in the living room the way she usually does. I expect that's because someone had moved all the furniture about in the downstairs rooms and taken away the wall that used to be between them, if you can believe such a thing. It made me blink when I saw it, I have to admit, but that *is* what they'd done. But it didn't matter because the treats we'd been promised were on the dining room table, which seemed to have grown to twice its size and was absolutely piled with food, prawns, chicken legs, salmon. To be honest there was more of it than we could possibly eat, but it was so kind of her to leave it for us like that, we jumped up on the table and started eating at once.

It was quite hard to find room to stand in, because there were so many other things on that table besides the food, piles of plates, a basket full of knives and forks, vases of flowers and bottles everywhere. We had to push things to one side to make a space. But we're nothing if not resourceful, we cats, and it didn't take us long. Kitty pulled a chicken leg from the plate and jumped down onto the carpet to eat it there, where she had more room, but I started on the prawns, because they are well and away my favourites. The trouble was whoever'd set the food out had put them in little swirls of pastry like shells and it was quite difficult to pick them out neatly, without getting pastry all over my fur. I did it, of course, and I did it neatly, because, not that I brag, I'm a very fastidious eater, but it took a long time. Kitty had demolished three chicken legs before I'd finished with the first plate, and by then we were ready to move on to the salmon, which was arranged in the middle of the table, with slices of cucumber all over it and a black olive where its eye had been. We sorted that out quite quickly because the cucumber was easy to push to one side. And the fish was delicious. We ate it slowly, partly to savour every mouthful but mostly because that was the only way we could eat when our bellies were so full of food already. Jenny was going to be so pleased to see how much we'd enjoyed it.

As I was cleaning my whiskers and Kitty was licking her paws, there was the sound of the front door being opened and then a rush of noisy air and lots of giggling and the crowd were back with Jenny and Sandyman swept up in the middle of them all. I don't know what they'd been doing while they were out but Jenny's pretty white suit and her hat were covered in little bits of coloured paper. It was even in her hair. And Sandyman was speckled with it too. They all came to a sudden halt in the space where the wall had been and stared at us, as if they couldn't believe their eyes. As well they might.

'Oh my dear good God!' Jenny said. 'Look at it, Malc. Just look at it. That was our wedding breakfast.'

And the rest of them drew in their breath and said. 'Good heavens!' and 'I say!'

'Doan' you worry,' Leroy's voice said, and there he was stepping out of the crowd and ambling up to Jenny in his lovely easy way. 'I sort it. Doan' you worry. Have a little drink. Give me five minutes an' it'll all be right as rain.'

'How could he do such a thing?' Jenny said.

'He a cat,' Leroy said. 'He like prawn, an' salmon. Doan you worry. We get it clean an' clear for you, no time.'

Jenny was looking at me, half smiling. 'Oh Cat!' she said. 'What am I to do with you?' I wasn't quite sure what she meant so I gave her my hopefully loving look. And that made her smile at me and then Sandyman gave her a hug and Feathers started to hand round glasses full of champagne and they were all laughing and talking.

'Well we'll never be able to say this wasn't a memorable wedding,' Sandyman said as he and Jenny clinked their glasses together.

'Here's to Cat!' she said.

I knew she'd be pleased.

Printed in Great Britain
by Amazon